HEARTS OF FIRE

F.R. WILSON

DETROIT INK
PUBLISHING

HEARTS OF FIRE

F.R. WILSON

HEARTS OF FIRE

Published by Detroit Ink Publishing

Detroit, Michigan

Cover Design by Sydgrafix

Detroit, Michigan

Publisher's Note:

This is a work of fiction. All events and characters in this story are solely the product of the author's imagination. Any similarities between characters and situations presented in this book to any individuals, living or dead, are purely coincidental.

Printed in the United States of America

ISBN: 978-0-99995739-5-2

ALSO BY F.R. WILSON

Cast A Long Shadow

Planet Eden

CHAPTER 1

*T*alia moved her arms, dipping and swaying them like a bird in flight. The air around her began to warm and hum. The stone walls of the turret seemed to expand and contract, as if the room were breathing in and out. Vibrations rippled through the floor, causing the glass vials and bottles on the tables in her father's laboratory to rattle and shake. Books tumbled from their perches on the shelves. Charts and maps on the wall flapped like wings. Moisture collected on the windows like a sweaty brow. The smell of something burning tickled Talia's nose. The whole turret seemed to be threatening to dislodge itself from the castle as if it would shoot into the air and explode like fireworks.

"Easy now. Slowly. Don't rush it." Her father warned watching attentively over her shoulder. "Gently, Talia. Visualize what you're doing. See the end result. You want to guide the forces around you. Don't gather them too fast. Stay in control. Feel it. Hold it. Don't let it over power you."

"Yes, Father," Talia answered, her breathing becoming rapid and shallow. Beads of sweat formed above her brows. Talia licked the salty moisture from above her lips. Her arms moved faster. The nerves in her fingers and hands began to tingle and go numb. She grunted from the strain of controlling the growing force. "Father," she whispered, a plea entering her voice.

"Too fast Talia. Slow it down. You'll lose it."

The pull of the mounting power caused her to wobble on her feet. "Father, I can't keep up with it. It's too strong. I can't hold it." Panic started to take hold.

"You can do it, Talia. You must believe in yourself abilities, in your abilities."

"It's too much. I can't." Her head jerked to face him. "I'm scared, Father. What do I do?" The power continued to grow as she struggled to contain it. Her arms spread wide like a chambermaid loaded down with laundry. She felt her muscles strain and burn from the effort.

"Concentrate, Talia. Keep your focus. Don't be afraid," he shouted.

"Father, please." She cried.

Talleon reached in to help her. A bolt of energy, bright as lightning, arched and struck him in the chest. He rocketed straight up into the air and bounced off the ceiling. Talleon crashed onto the stone floor like a bird shot on the wing.

"Father, Father!" Talia screamed. A wall of flames rose up, engulfing her. The magic surged through her like boiling water. Talia was both terrified and amazed. She felt as she had never felt before, both powerful and frightened.

Stepping forward, she reached for her father. The room began to spin. The air moved around her in a whirlwind. The power shot through her body; overwhelming her. Talia struggled to stay on her feet, to help her fallen father. The hurricane of wind and flame danced about her. The familiar surrounding became a blur. She gasped. Everything went black.

*T*alia collapsed on the bed in tears. The memory was too raw, too fresh. Tears of guilt mingled with those of lost and regret.

The door creaked open. Talia jumped, only relaxing when Alana peeked into the room. Sniffling, she wiped her eyes and returned to her task. Opening a satchel, in went two dresses, an ivory comb, a brush, and a book of her father's spells. She lingered over an iridescent blue crystal amulet; her mother's amulet. A sad weak smile crossed her lips. Stories told of her mother played through her mind. Talia stroked the gemstone before tying the braided leather string around her neck.

"I didn't mean to disturb you." Alana said shuffling into the room.

"It's alright. I thought you were..." She shook her head. "It doesn't matter."

"So, you're really leaving?" She frowned. "But why, Talia?"

Talia ignored the question and closed her bag. "You can have the rest." She pointed to the assortment of dresses and petticoats laid out like a bouquet of wild flowers.

"Most of these things were given to you by the prince."

" I don't want them!" Talia snapped. "If you won't take them give them to the other girls. They love these frills and ruffles."

Alana drew back at the sharpness of her reply. "You can't leave, Talia," Her voice was shaking. "Where will you go? Now that your father is dea... I mean gone." Her face flushed. "You don't have any other family. Who will look after you? Who will protect you? How will you live? You'll be a woman alone in the world."

"I'll take care of myself," Talia insisted, pausing and taking a deep breath to fortify herself. "I'll be fine. I have my magic. My father taught me well." She turned away hoping Alana wouldn't see what she was hiding. Talia raised her chin to conceal the doubt in her voice. "There is nothing left for me here. If I stay I'll be forced into a life I don't want. I will not be chained to a cooking pot and a cradle. Forced to sit like one of the court hounds and come when called."

"If you marry the prince you won't have to worry about all that. You'll have servants and all the best the kingdom can offer."

"I won't have him. I am not suited to be the royal brood mare. He doesn't love me. I don't love him." She snapped. "Thangor is cruel and arrogant. He thinks only of what he wants. My life would not be my own. I want to live as I choose, not as someone commands me to."

Alana gave her an annoyed look. "You've always been so proud and picky. Prince Thangor is the most sought-after man in the kingdom. He will be king one day. Any woman should be proud to have his favor."

"He doesn't have mine and I don't want his." Talia sat resting her hands in her lap and stared out the window at the rising sun. "I want to do things and see things like my father did when he was young. I want a life of wonder and adventure. There is nothing to wonder about here. The biggest adventure here is what the cook will make for dinner tonight. No, there's nothing for me here. I want to find out what I can be, what I can do, not have it dictated for me. Father always said I was more than I realized I was. I want to find out if that is true."

Alana fondled the ruffles on a purple silk ball gown. Her expression softened as her eyes teared up. "Talia, don't go. I'll miss you terribly." Her voice faded to a whimper. "There's no one like you. I don't really fit in with the other girls. I'll be all alone. Besides..." She cracked a small smile. "I want you to be my maid of honor."

"Alana, Pauna finally asked you?"

Alana's face lit up like a candle. She bounced her head up and down like a ball on a string. The two young women giggled and hugged.

"I'm so happy for you, Alana. I know you two will be very happy. He's a good man."

"See you can't go. Who will stand up for me?"

"I'm sorry, Alana. I wish I could, but I have got to go. I hate I can't stand up for you. But, if I don't leave now I may never get another chance to escape. I'll miss you. But, I can't stay." She reached out and took her hands. A devilish smile crossed her lips. She tilted her head. "I bet that handsome soon-to-be husband of yours will keep you so busy you won't even know I'm gone."

"Oh pooh." Alana waved off the comment. "He's just a man. A woman needs other women to talk to. Men are not understanding in that way."

"Oh, he understands you plenty," Talia raised her brows. Alana's face reddened and they both laughed as only young women in the bloom of life can.

"You not being there will spoil the wedding." Alana protested pushing a dress out of the way and plopping down on the bed. "I was so looking forward to my best friend being my bridesmaid." She hung her head and pouted.

"I know, but I really can't stay. Things have become too complicated and uncomfortable for me here. Please understand. This is hard enough. I have to do this."

The young women hugged, and Talia wiped tears from Alana's eyes. "I must be going before I am missed. I have far to travel before night." Kissing her friends' cheek, she left the castle and began her trek toward the village.

One last look at the castle as she wound her way past the stables. Talia saw someone peering from a perch on the battlements. The figure was shrouded in black and clung to the shadows like a swamp rat. The hairs on the back of her neck bristled. He lowered his hood and nodded. It was Cannullus. Even at a distance his crooked smirk was unnerving. Her footsteps quickened matching the rapid beating of her heart.

"Your secret is safe with me." Cannullus spoke slowly, emphasizing every word. "As long as I am the magician at the court. No one will know what you did." He paused smiling like a jackal. "I can be a great friend to you, Talia. If you would consider it, we could be much more. As your intended, I could do many things for you." His eyes were groping her as if they were his long thin fingers.

"What about Thangor?" She asked more as a threat than a question. "He expects..."

Cannullus stepped forward and took her hand. "What he expects can change." A twisted grin crossed his lips. "If you chose it, together we could be the power in Mandoria."

Talia snatched her hand away; anger providing a morsel of courage. "I will not have Thangor. I will not have you. Look elsewhere for your accomplice. My life will not be something that can be bartered for or conspired to get."

Cannullus expanded his smile. His words were clear and singular. "You may find it difficult to remain here with such sad and tragic memories surrounding you. There will be those who are not so understanding as I. You would be vulnerable standing so..." The grin eclipsed his face "alone." A hint of accusation and threat was in his voice. "Things have a way of surfacing. I don't know what may happen if certain things are revealed. The telling may not present you in the fairest light. After all it is just your word that it was an accident. There are those that could make an argument for malice." He leaned in to whisper in her ear. "Think of it Talia, the consequences could be severe."

"We sometimes disagreed. Our opinions of my future were different. I would never harm my father. The magic just got away from me and..."

He placed a flat palm to his chest. "I'm sure it was an accident, but..." Cannullus dragged out the words. "The king may not see it that way. He may not believe in your innocence. His majesty has always been suspicious of magic and those who possess it. If he didn't have such a long history with your father, magic might already be outlawed." Talia knew there was no longer a place for her in the castle. Disappearing into the morning mist was the best thing she could do. Turning from the castle she put its existence in her past.

CHAPTER 2

*T*he horse she received for her 16th birthday neighed and whinnied when she entered the stables. Talia always came with a bag of his favorite treat, green apples. "I need a friend, Apple-jack. I have to leave. If you're with me I won't feel so alone."

Talia rode to the blacksmith shop. Barnabas was busy hammering at his anvil. Thick smoke, like black balls of cotton, drifted on the air. Sparks danced around the puffs of smoke like small lighting storms, twinkling against the ash filled air. He removed his foot from the bellow and laid down his hammer when she entered.

The large bear of a man stood with his fists on his hips, giving her a disapproving glare. "You're really leaving then?" His voice, deep from years of breathing the heavy air, echoed as if it came from a cave. The words were more a statement than a question.

Feeling transported back to being a young girl, Talia tugged at her cloak and nodded yes. "I couldn't leave without saying goodbye to you. You've been family to me; like an uncle to me. As father's best friend, you know better than anyone that I must do this. My mother and brother are out there. Now that Father is gone they are my only family. Except you, I mean, Uncle Barnabas." She blushed at the omission. "I mean to find them." Jetting out a determined chin. "I need to find them."

"You are surely your father's daughter," He coughed, dislodging a puff of soot from his beard. Barnabas' rough features softened as his eyes widened in a plea. "Talia, think again, my girl. Your mother's a..." he looked around making sure no one would hear. "A Centaur."

"I know that. It doesn't change anything. Even if I was taken away as a babe to protect me from the Centaurs, that was then. This is now. I'm not a helpless infant anymore."

"But, Talia you can't really expect them to except you with open arms. Centaurs and humans aren't friends."

"My mother and father weren't enemies." She insisted. "They loved each other. I know when I find them things will be different. I am part Centaur. They will not turn me away."

"I'm not so sure that will make a difference. You don't know much about Centaurs. They're a rowdy bunch." He held out his hands like a beggar. "At least change your mind and let me go with you. I'll close up the shop and we can leave on the morrow."

Barnabas yanked off his apron and began dusting himself off. A cloud of dark dust and ash filled the air, causing him to cough and causing her to sneeze.

Talia waved a path through the smoky curtain and placed a hand on his arm. "Barnabas, please let's not do this. We've discussed this already. I love you and I appreciate your concern for me, but I need to do this, and do it on my own. I have no future here. I must go. I'll be all right. Don't worry." Talia's emerald eyes twinkled with the hint of tears.

"Don't worry?" Barnabas said, shaking his head. "I've worried about you ever since your father brought you home. Such a tiny helpless thing you were. I worried when you cried or fell or got sick. I worried when the other kids teased you about your ears or the bumps on your head.

Don't worry." He laughed. "I don't think I can develop that talent now." He folded his massive bulk around her. "Since Talleon is no longer with us I worry for the both of us now. Your magic may not be enough Talia. I know that your father schooled you but..."

She stepped out of his embrace with smudged cheeks. "Please try to understand. I'm not a child. I know what I'm doing."

"Reconsider," he tried one last time. "You can stay and serve as the court sorceress like your father did." He brushed her sooty cheeks with an equally dirty cloth, increasing the smug.

"That job belongs to Cannullus now. He fought Father for it all my life. Now that he has it, nothing will convince him to give it up. Besides, I don't want it. Being at the castle doesn't mean anything to me now that Father isn't there. My destiny lies elsewhere."

"That conniving rascal Cannullus doesn't have half your talent. Why he's..."

"It doesn't matter, Barnabas. I've decided. I'm leaving." Talia stiffened her back and tried to look taller. *"I've got to leave. I can't stay even if I wanted to. I couldn't bear it if you found out what I did,"* She thought.

He nodded his surrender and hugged her again and wiped her cheeks again like a doting mother. Barnabas went to the door and grabbed the horse by his reins.

"You take care of her, Applejack. She's headstrong. She thinks she doesn't need us any longer. So, you'll have to be cautious for the both of you." The horse looked at him with dismissive eyes as if to say, "don't tell me how to do my job."

Then he shifted his head, ignoring the blacksmith all together. Barnabas stood in the doorway, his arms crossed and his eyes full of worry. "Be safe, my girl," he whispered, as he watched her ride out of town and disappear into the morning mist.

On the stone bridge, outside of town, Talia encountered Prince Thangor sitting crossed legged on the back of a speckled roan. He was smirking and casually examining his fingernails. There was little doubt he had been waiting for her to arrive. Determined not to let him have the satisfaction of seeing any frustration, Talia continued riding without changing her pace.

Thangor was handsome beneath his layers of showy attire. He was rich, young, and the most eligible bachelor in the land. His overt attention to his grooming and dress made him look like a child playing dress up. He paraded about in gaudy colored uniforms full of stripes, epaulets, and crests. His pointed features were made comical by the precise angular mustache and goatee he sported because they looked more like they were painted on then grown naturally. Rapacious brown eyes leered from under the brim of a feathered hat that sat on a mop of black heavily oiled hair, and he had the glower of someone overly satisfied with himself plastered on his face.

"Going somewhere?" His tone was more an accusation than an inquiry.

"Obviously," she said, looking at him with contempt as she attempted to go around his horse. Her emerald eyes blazed hard and clear. Thangor shifted his horse's position to continue blocking the narrow bridge. Talia softly but firmly asked: "May I pass, please."

"That's better," he said smiling, flashing a perfect row of alabaster teeth that gleamed like polished stones. "I don't remember you asking my permission to go traveling? As assistant to the former court sorcerer, your presence is required and vital."

"I am a free woman, Thangor. I do not need your permission to go where I please."

"I'm sorry. I don't think you understand who the royal is here. You are free as long as I decree that you are free. Besides you are privy to certain court secrets that must be protected."

"Secrets?" She chuckled. "What secrets? That the court wine is watered down? That the tax scales are weighted? Or maybe that you, despite all your medals and awards, have never been near a battle?"

"Oh, how I would miss that delightful sense of humor if you weren't around." He said with a sarcastic shake of the head.

"Am I a servant? Am I to be considered property of the court? A slave?"

"Not a slave, but," he gloated. "a special subject. A very special subject. And as my special subject it is my duty to protect you, which I cannot do if you are off traipsing through the countryside. Now that Talleon isn't with us any longer I feel a certain extra responsibility to look after you. As my future consort, it will not do for you to be off..."

"Thangor," she interrupted. "What do you really want?" He leaned toward her grinning, staring with the eyes of a hungry dog. "Just how explicit do you want me to be?"

"Don't you have some villagers to harass or some chamber maid to ravage? I wouldn't want to keep you from your royal duties."

"Careful now," he wagged a well-manicured finger at her. "That biting wit of yours can go a bit too far."

"I am sorry, your highness," she said faking a bow. "If you will allow me to pass I will take my biting wit out of your presence."

"Oh, I will have such fun taming that independent spirit of yours."

"There are so many who would fight for your favor. Why do you persist in honoring me with your attentions?"

"Let's just say I enjoy a challenge."

"Thangor, I've told you I don't want to be your consort or your queen. I don't want to live in the castle. I don't love you."

"My dear, I don't remember what you want ever being the point. Besides in time you will surrender to my charms. Trust me there will come a time when you will beg to be in my good graces." He waved his hand as if brushing away crumbs. "Go on your little adventure. Grieve for your poor departed father." He raised a finger. "But, don't go too far. I will expect you back, and soon. If you aren't, I will come and retrieve you. Accept it Talia, you are mine and I will have you anyway I want, as my queen or not, it doesn't matter to me." He galloped away in a cloud of dust and laughter.

Thangor had once been her favorite companion. They grew up side by side in the palace. As children, they played and laughed together as equals. Running through the halls of the castle, romping in the gardens making mischief as happy children do. In those days, she did love him and thought him the cleverest creature ever. Her differences didn't seem to matter to him. He showered her with attention and affection and she returned it happily. In their early teens, Thangor was sent away to be schooled and groomed for his role as the next ruler of Mandoria.

When he returned, he was changed. His manner had become haughty and arrogant. The happy boy she had known was replaced with a callous young man who lauded his station and authority over everyone for his own amusement.

Talia knew he didn't love her. He wanted her only for her abilities and the advantages it would provide him as the next ruler. "Magic," her father had warned her, "can do great good, but in the wrong hands it can do great ill. Be wary how you yield your gifts. Do not let those in power make you powerless by controlling you. If you aren't making your own decisions no matter how powerful you are, you are a slave." The warning had been taken to heart. When Thangor returned and started his proclamations of affection to her she saw through his pretenses.

CHAPTER 3

$\mathcal{A}$fter traveling for miles, Talia was still consumed by her anger against Thangor. Three pairs of roguish eyes tracking her went unnoticed, until they stood across the road blocking her path. The trio of dirty ragged men leaned on fighting poles, their mouths drawn back in devilish smiles displaying a severe loss of teeth, with green and yellow stains on those that remained.

"What do we have here?" said the first one, standing just in front of the others and marking him as the leader.

"It appears to be a lost lamb looking to get sheared," answered the second, as they all three united in laughter.

"You wouldn't be able to help three poor gentlemen down on their luck, could you little lamb?" asked the third with a boyish giggle.

"Gentlemen?" She asked in a mocking tone sitting erect in her saddle. "I think you are being very generous with the term."

The leader angled his head. "A lamb with a sharp tongue. I think we best be careful, gents. She might cut us with it." laughed the leader, unsheathing his knife and fixing her with a contemptuous glare. "Now why don't you come down here and act like a respectful little lamb. You may escape with your respectability and your life." He spit at the horses' hooves.

"The kingdom does not respond kindly to bandits." Talia said.

"Bandits?" fawned the leader bringing his hand to his chest as if he was offended by the suggestion. "We are not bandits. We are businessmen who happen to enjoy the country air. Toll collector for the crown, we are."

"Yeah," agreed the second. "That's right. We're toll collectors for the crown." All three nodded and shared a laugh.

"I think not," said Talia, raising her hand just as one of the bandits lunged for the reins. Applejack balked, rearing up, sending Talia crashing to the ground. The bandits retreated from the flailing hooves. Misspent magic popped and crackled in the air. Dancing sparks and the smell of singed hair spread through the air. Applejack bolted down the road back toward the town.

"She's a Witch!" one yelled. "Kill her." They rushed forward, knives and fighting sticks raised. Talia managed to rise to a sitting position and cast a spell that created a blast of wind pushing the men backwards. She rose to her feet rubbing the back of her head.

"We'll gonna gut you witch, burn your bones, and cast your ashes to the wind," said the leader. They circled her, swinging and jabbing at her with their fighting poles. Two of the bandits rushed forward.

Talia extended her arms, palms up and pedaled them forward. "Not a Witch," she exclaimed. "A Sorceress." A blinding flash of energy struck the two in the chest, sending them somersaulting into the air. They crashed into a tree and landed with a thud, lying unconscious on the ground. Talia turned just as the third bandit fell face down at her feet. She looked up and met the smiling soft brown eyes of a Satyr. He smiled, standing over the fallen man holding a large branch.

The Satyr looked about her age and was slightly shorter than she. His two short horns made her think of her own horn buds. The Satyr had a thin wispy beard, short, curly, sandy-colored hair, and small cloven ears. The twinkle in his eyes matched perfectly with his welcoming smile and chipmunk cheeks.

Talia smiled and bowed. "Thank you, sir. I'm afraid I was out flanked."

"Three against one didn't seem very fair to me." he replied, pointing down the road at Talia's speeding horse.

"I'm afraid you've lost your horse. He doesn't appear to have the heart for fighting." Talia looked down the road at Applejack and sighed as she continued to rub the back of her head. He surveyed the prone men. "I think we should get away from here before they wake up." He paused.

"They will wake up, won't they? You didn't kill them, did you? I mean, I wouldn't blame you if you did. But..."

"No, I didn't kill them. They will recover, maybe with a few aches and bruises, but alive."

"Oh good." he sighed. "I wouldn't want to kill anyone or be part of killing anyone. It's not that I'm saying you're a bad person or a killer. I just meant that it's good they aren't dead even if they are bad men."

"My name is Talia." she said, "And who is my hero?"

The Satyr looked around and smiled. "Oh, you mean me."

He pointed at himself. "I'm Hanar, Hanar Knoll. I'm a Satyr. I live here in the forest." Realizing he was still holding the branch, he threw it away as if it had turned into a snake.

Hanar flicked his head. "Come on we better go. I don't think it will be a good idea to be around when they wake up."

Talia looked down the road. Applejack was lost in a trail of dust. She looked at the three dirty bandits laying on the ground like fallen trees. She nodded, stepped over her would be attacker and followed Hanar into the woods.

CHAPTER 4

*W*alking through the woods, Talia was amazed how Hanar's hooves made no sound as if they never touched the ground. His goat-like legs were lean and muscular. She was delighted to see how nibble and sure-footed he was and how gracefully he traversed the trail. A fuzzy coat of hair covered his lower body. The hair bunched up and was shorn from the top of his pants and at to the hem. She smiled at the stubby tail that stuck out from a hole in the back of his pants. The tail twitched with each step.

His top half was smooth and covered with a fine mesh of hair that glistened with a thin layer of sweat. Hanar wore no shirt, only a multi-color vest tied together with a braided cord. He cleared a path for her making sure to only bend and not break the branches or up root the greenery. "These woods are my home. I know every tree and rock for miles. This place is part of me."

"Have you lived here long?" she asked.

"Almost eleven turns of the seasons."

"You live here with your family?"

Hanar lowered his head. "I have no family. Not anymore. The Wolfmen killed my mother and father ten summers ago. They invaded our homeland. We were attacked. My parents fought them off, sacrificing themselves so I could get away."

He placed a hand to his ear. "I can still hear my mother crying out, 'Run Hanar, run,' as they fought for their lives." His voice became weak and thin. "I was very young. I was so scared. I ran like the demons of the underworld were after me. I kept going until I couldn't run anymore. When I collapsed, I was in this place. I waited and waited, praying my parents would find me. They never came.

"Eventually, I knew they would never come. I have lived here alone ever since." His expression was blank and his eyes cloudy as he replayed the memory.

"I'm sorry. It must be hard to be so alone."

He snapped out of his trance and managed a small smile. "I'm not alone. I have many friends. All the animals of the forest are my family. We live together, play together, and protect each other. So, you see I'm never alone." Hanar stopped and looked to the sky. "It's getting late in the day we'll never make it back to Mandoria before dark, and Alserra is too far away. You can stay with me tonight. I'll take you there tomorrow."

"If it wouldn't be too much trouble I would like that. I'm afraid all I have now are the clothes on my back and my cloak. I don't want to sleep out in the open."

"It'll be nice to have someone to talk to who can talk back for a change. Owls, squirrels, and deer are nice, but they don't say much. Lots of grunts and squeaks, but not many words. My home is not too far. It's this way." He said leading her deeper into the thickening darkness of the forest.

They came to a tree larger around than any Talia had ever seen before. Hanar motioned for her to follow as he disappeared into an indention in the tree. She cautiously followed, wound a turn, and entered into a large room. The tree was hollow in the middle. The space was furnished with a short large stump for a table, a dug-out trunk for a chair, a sleep mat of straw and cloth, and a large pit of stones with a fire burning in it. A small wooden barrel with a lid held water. When you looked up you could see the sky through an opening in the middle of the roof where the tree shot up into the clouds. The smoke trickled up and escaped into the canopy of branches.

"This is my home. You are safe here. Consider this your home for tonight." He smiled with pride.

"This is wonderful. I've never seen anything like it," Talia said, walking in a circle to take it all in. "I will be very pleased to spend the night here."

"I'll go and get us something to eat. There are lots of fruit trees and wonderful berries around here. I'll be back soon." He disappeared out the opening.

Talia sat and removed her shoes. She thought about Barnabus. He would be worried when Applejack returned without her. Maybe she should go back and assure him she was all right. *If I go back Thangor will not let me leave again. He would never let me forget my failed attempt to leave. No, I can't risk going back. And there was Cannullus to consider. What would he do? Would he ruin her or try to control her? I can't risk it. I wouldn't allow myself to be trapped in Mandoria*, she thought. *My horse; my bag. I have nothing, and I still have to find the Centaurs village.*

Talia held her head in her hands and tried not to fall victim to her waning confidence. *This has not been a good beginning.* The world had gotten so much more difficult since her father's death.

"Father," she whispered. "You always said there was a way to do anything. But, I have nothing. I have lost you and now I've lost all my possessions. The only things I have left are the clothes on my back and mother's amulet." She wrapped her hand around the amulet and closed her eyes. The doubt and fear just kept growing.

Maybe Barnabus was right, she thought. *Maybe I should just forget this. What if I make it to the village and they turn me away? What would I do then? Become a beggar wandering the land selling my services as a Sorceress to wealthy merchants. No, magic shouldn't be for sale.* She plopped down on the stump with a sigh, her resolve faltering.

If marrying Thangor is my only other choice maybe I should just accept it and stop fooling myself. Maybe life doesn't hold anything different for me. Even if Cannullus makes good on his threats, as queen I might be protected.

Talia stood and circled the room. *No, this is what I should do. This is the right thing. There's nothing for me in Mandoria.*

Talia pulled her cloak tight around herself, giving herself a hug of reassurance. *I have to go on. I know that my mother and brother will be happy to see me.* All her life Talia had dreamt of them. Talleon would speak so little of them. Sometimes he'd refuse to talk of them at all. Whenever he did talk about them, he'd end up feeling so low and maudlin. She knew he missed them too.

"Can't we go find them?" Talia would ask. Talleon would just shake his head and change the subject. This adventure was her idea, her decision, and her responsibility.

A gray squirrel with a white spot in the center of his forehead climbed down the wall and sat on the table opposite her. "Hello there, little fellow. Aren't you cute?" She held out her hand. He smelled it and returned to sitting and staring. "What's your name?" she asked.

"That's Capell," said Hanar, silently entering the room like a puff of air. "He was one of my first friends when I came here. We've grown up together."

"He's adorable," Talia said.

"Be careful," he whispered. "He's a thief. If you don't look out, he'll take whatever he can get his little paws on."

As if on cue, Capell grabbed a mouth full of the berries Hanar had just sat down and scampered up the wall and onto the branches of the tree.

"I think Capell has a family to feed these days." Hanar said. They laughed as they watched him disappearing through the opening at the top.

Talia ate fruit while Hanar warmed some water. He put several leaves into the hot water and handed Talia a wooden cup with the brew in it. She smelled it. "Bramberry tea. I love this."

"I see you know your herbs. My people learn all about them from the time we are very small."

"The study of plants was part of my training."

"Who was your teacher?" Hanar asked.

"My father, Talleon, he was the court Sorcerer at Mandoria. He taught me to be a Sorceress like him. I owe all that I know to him."

"I was as surprised as those men when you did your magic. It was very impressive. Too bad the horse messed everything up." He hunched his shoulders. "Is your father still in Mandoria?"

She buried her face in her cup. "He died a short while ago."

"I'm sorry. Does that mean you're alone like me?"

"Not quite. I'm on my way to find my mother and my brother. They live in the Centaurs' village." Hanar's eyes widened with fright.

"What's wrong?" she asked.

"Satyrs avoid Centaurs. They capture my kind and use us as slaves or keep us as pets."

"As slaves and pets? That's horrible." He nodded a silent assent.

"I'm sorry about your mother and brother. How long have they been slaves to the Centaurs?"

"No" she said hesitantly. "You don't understand. My mother and brother aren't slaves to the Centaurs." She pulled back her long black hair and revealed her cloven ears. She lowered her head, parted her wavy tresses and showed him her horn buds and said in a soft voice full of apprehension, "They are Centaurs, part of the clan. You see, I'm part Human and part Centaur."

Hanar stiffened and leaned away from her. Talia recognized the look. She felt drawn back to when she was a young girl; back to the time when she had to learn to live with the rejection of being different. Back to the fear and revulsion she saw in peoples' eyes. Back to the shame and loneliness of not being wanted or belonging. Back before her father taught her that her differences weren't a curse. Before she understood that she was the product of love and had nothing to be ashamed of.

"How is that possible?" He asked in amazement. "Is it a curse? Is it magic?"

Relaxing at his curiosity she said, "I guess you could say in a way its magic. Yes. It was magic. It was love." Hanar moved to a sitting position in front of her like a child waiting for a bedtime story. Wide eyed he rested his head on his hand and leaned in waiting attentively.

"When my father was a young Sorcerer he went out in the world to learn more about his craft. One day he happened upon a battlefield. From the trees, he watched as the Centaurs and the Wolfmen warred against each other. After a ferocious battle, he walked the fields lamenting the carnage. A beautiful young female Centaur caught his eye. He remembered seeing her during the battle. She was skilled and magnificent. He was very impressed with her abilities and courage. I think he fell in love with her at that moment. Her name was Cyrenia. She was badly wounded, but not dead. He took her to the secluded cave where he had been living during his studies. Being skilled with herbs and elixirs he tended to her injuries.

"As she recovered, she fell in love with him as well. Eventually, my twin brother, Cyron, and I were born. I was mostly human, and my brother was mostly Centaur. Our parents knew they couldn't stay hidden forever. And they couldn't stay together. A decision had to be made. It was a hard one. They knew there was a chance they would never see each other again. They agreed that when they parted I should go with father and Cyron should stay with our mother. Now that my father is gone, I have decided it is time to find them and reunite our family."

"You can't go there. They'll enslave you or kill you. You may have the blood of a Centaur, but you are not one of them. They won't accept you."

"I don't believe that. My mother and brother won't allow that."

"Talia, the Centaurs may not be at war with the Humans, but they don't like them. I don't think they like anyone who isn't a Centaur. I know they are at war with the Wolfmen. They're mortal enemies. They have been fighting a long time. I've seen them." His voice was shaky. "I don't know which one is worse. You shouldn't go anywhere near either of them." His eyes were wide as saucers.

"Neither the Centaurs nor the Wolfmen like Humans. Your father never took you there, did he?" She shook her head.

"That must mean something. He knew. Even with your magic you won't be safe." He shook his head. "They won't accept you."

"Hanar, I've thought about it. I won't believe that. My heart tells me this is the right thing to do. They are my family and I'm going." She crossed her arms defiantly. "My mind is made up." Softening her voice, she asked. "Would you lead me to the Centaur village?"

Hanar's expression grew wild and he shook his head no. "I won't go anywhere near there."

"Then will you at least point me in the right direction?"

Hanar crawled away from her and curled up in the corner, his eyes full of fear. The tips of his pointed ears flicked with a nervous twitch. He turned his back to her and buried his head between his trembling legs. Talia sighed and moved to the straw mat, wrapping herself in her cloak. The exhaustion of the day's events took hold of her. Worry and frustration did the rest. She drifted off to a troubled sleep.

CHAPTER 5

*W*hen Talia awoke the next morning, Hanar was gone. She stepped outside and stretched the sleep from her body. The sun was just creeping up over the horizon. Forest animals were busy waking up and getting on with their day. Capell showed up looking for an easy breakfast.

"Good morning, Capell," she said bending down to stroke his chubby cheeks. "I'm sorry there isn't anything left. I'm afraid we ate it all last evening." He gave her a displeased squeak and scurried away across the forest floor.

The peace and the beauty of the forest calmed her. Talia thought of the long walks with her father in the woods around Mandoria when he would give her lessons on the plants and animals, and describing the herbs, roots, and leaves they encountered. He had her make and study long lists of the many uses and properties of each.

"Father," she said looking into the clear azure sky. "I'm so sorry for everything that happened. I promise to not let anything like that ever happen again. I will heed your words and be more careful." She closed her eyes. "I wish you were here. I miss you so much."

Hanar appeared with an arm full of fruits. "We'll leave as soon as we have something to eat," he said tossing her an apple.

"You'll take me to the Centaurs' village?"

"I can't let you go alone. You'll get lost. Besides, I didn't save you just so you could end in worst shape." He smiled as her grateful eyes blinked thanks at him over the apple.

An hour later Hanar had packed his bag, woven out of collop leaves, and vines and they were off through the forest.

"The Centaurs' village is about four or five days' journey to the west through the forest. We'll have to be very careful about three days in because we will come very close to the Wolfmen's territory. They make raids into other's lands. We have to keep an eye out for foraging packs."

His voice grew soft. "My old home, the one I shared with my parents, is near their borders. I haven't had the courage to return since...since." He swallowed the words.

"I understand," Talia said laying a hand on his shoulder. "Hanar, I can't thank you enough for doing this. I know that it is hard for you to go there."

"It's all right." His expression brightened. "My father used to say: 'Hanar if you haven't tried it how do you know you can't do it?'"

They walked and talked, sharing stories of their lives and families. Talia tried to keep pace with Hanar. He bounded through the forest with such ease, at home with every grove, thicket, or untraveled path they encountered.

Talia attempted to match his practiced steps. She stumbled and struggled, tripping over stones and getting tangled in vines and briars. Hard as she tried, her city ways shone through. Noticing that she was lagging behind him, Hanar made excuses to make frequent stops so she could catch up and rest.

Detouring for water at a small stream, Talia removed her shoes and soaked her sore feet. Her shoes and clothes were made for riding not hiking. She dangled her toes in the cool water, let out a deep sigh, and laid back exhausted.

Hanar removed some fruit from his bag for them and filled his water skin. "Talia, what made you decide to learn magic?"

"What do you mean?"

"I mean you're Human, not like a Fairy or a Dragon. They are born magical. Humans have to learn magic. So, what made you decide to learn to be a Sorceress?"

"I didn't decide. I was born into it too. Magic is all I've ever known. My father said that some people are born with a gift for magic. He said I was born to it and that's why it comes so naturally to me. It's second nature to me."

"Do you feel magical?"

"I don't know. I never thought about it that way. Magic just feels right. It's what I do. It's who I am."

*T*hat night and the next they slept around a small fire. Talia wove a ward of protection around them to keep animals away and to warn them of unseen dangers. Try as she might, she could not ward against the dreams of seeing her father broken and bloody on the floor of his laboratory. She would wake up sweating and holding a scream in her throat.

On the morning of the third day they happened upon a slaughtered deer. It had been torn apart. Blood and gore was smeared on the plants and the trees. Pieces of the animal had been tossed about staining the ground and surrounding foliage.

"Wolfmen," hissed Hanar. "They probably weren't even hunting. They did this for sport. They're leaving a sign and marking new territory." The disgust and fear were clear in his voice.

"Wolfmen are vicious and cruel, killing for the pleasure of it. Stay as quiet as possible. We have to be careful and not let them surprise us. Keep your eyes and ears open."

Hanar slowed the pace and moved with hesitation in his steps as he led Talia toward the area near his childhood home.

"We could take the long way and go around." Talia said.

"No, that would be even more dangerous. To do that would mean we'd be in their territory even longer. I can do this. We'll go the shortest way." His words were sure, but the quiver in his voice wasn't.

As they approached his childhood homestead, Hanar hardly recognized it. No trees were standing. All the majestic oaks, elm, sycamores, pines, willows, and maple that used to grow in his forest were reduced to stumps and charred rubble. The land was pockmarked with holes, covered with weeds, and decaying foliage. Even the ground looked used up and wasted away. Small patches of wild flowers struggled to peek their colorful heads out from under the destruction.

"This was our home," he whimpered slowly, closing his eyes against the crushing disappointment before him. "This was once a beautiful grove. Hollows much bigger than the one I live in now grew here." His eyes were blinded with tears. "The land was fertile and beautiful. Life bloomed on every inch of it. Many families lived in this place. Now there is no one and nothing."

He plopped to the ground. "The trees are gone, and the land is destroyed. I haven't seen another Satyr since I left this place. I guess...I'm the only thing left." He lowered his head. "I'm...I'm really alone."

"I'm so sorry, Hanar." Talia placed her hand on his shoulder. "You are not alone. I'm here and you'll see, Cyrenia and Cyron will welcome you too."

Hanar barely heard her words. "I didn't expect to find my parents." he whispered. "I at least thought the trees would still be here. I thought at least something of the past would have survived."

"Something did survive, Hanar." Talia grabbed him by the shoulders. "You did. Your parents wanted you to live. They sacrificed themselves so you would live. They live because you live. They live on in you." Hanar blinked back tears as he hung on her every word. "Maybe we can build a monument to them." Talia suggested.

Hanar brightened. "Could we?"

"Of course, we can. You gather some branches and I will get some vines and flowers. With a little work and a little magic, we'll build a fine memorial."

Bending branches and wrapping vines together, they created an arched trellis four hands tall and three hands wide. Talia decorated it with wild flowers, while Hanar wove a mat of grasses for it to rest on.

Hanar sat the arch on the mat in the middle of a large burned out stump that was once his home. He stepped back to admire it. The vines curled up and around the wooden frame. Bright rainbow-colored flowers intertwined each segment. The graceful arch of the structure made it look like it had grown that way. "It's beautiful. My parents would be so pleased."

He ran to her and wrapped her in an embrace. "Thank you, Talia. I would never have come here without you. I never would have had the courage. I never would have done this." He pointed to the arch.

"We're not finished yet."

"We're not? What are you going to do?"

"Stand over there," she ordered, "no, further away." She waved him further back. Hanar moved dozens of feet away.

"My father taught me this." Talia chanted some words, waved her arms, and laid her hands on the structure. She felt the pulsing of the magic as it swirled around her and flowed through her. Surging like wind through a tunnel, it wrapped around the trellis. The arch glowed red, then white, and began to buzz like a hive of bees. The colors grew brighter, exploding with brightness as if they were on fire. The wood, the vines, and the flowers hardened. In a matter of moments, it had become a colorful stone arch. Talia stepped back and approved her handiwork. "This will stand forever."

Hanar knelt before the structure. "For you, father. For you, mother. I love you. I miss you." Rising, he engulfed Talia again in a hug. "Thank you. You have made me so happy. It is so beautiful."

She smiled a sad smile remembering the one on her own father's grave. "What are friends for?" She finally managed to say.

They walked away, Hanar turning back every few feet to admire the monument until it could no longer be seen.

"We're too close to the Wolfmen's territory to risk a fire tonight. There are bound to be patrols or strays roaming around." Hanar said. The night was spent sitting in a tree camouflaged behind branches and leaves. A fine misty rain fell all through the night. Without the warmth of a fire to keep the chill and the dampness away, they huddled together shivering and using Talia's cloak and their body heat to keep warm. It was a miserable night. Not much sleep was had.

The next day Talia and Hanar skipped their morning meal and instead quickly moving out of the Wolfmen's range and into the domain of the Centaurs. Hanar's apprehension did not lessen, but instead seemed to grow with every step they took. Talia noticed and tried to ease his distress.

"Hanar, you have gotten me past the Wolfmen's land. We're not far from the Centaur village you should go back. I'll go on alone."

"No!" he snapped. "I will not leave you to be captured and enslaved. If this must be done, I will do it with you."

"But, you're putting yourself in great danger. You can't go into the village. They may not accept me, but you know they won't welcome you. I don't want to be the reason for you getting mistreated. I have no choice. I have to go, but you don't."

"I'll wait in the woods around the village. If something goes wrong I'll be nearby, maybe I can help. I have become very skilled at hiding in shadows. They won't know I'm there." He reached in his bag and gave her a small flute.

"This is a Satyr flute. Only Satyrs can hear the sound. If you blow into it, I will hear it and come to where you are."

"Please, my friend. I thank you for all you've done for me, but I could not bear it if something happened to you."

"No." he repeated again. "We go on together. After what you did for my mother and father they would never forgive me if I abandoned you." Hanar marched off with a reluctant Talia running to keep up.

CHAPTER 6

*O*n the morning of the fourth day, they reached the outskirts of the Centaur village. The smoke from chimneys in the settlement had been leading them for hours. The thatched roofs of dozens of houses could be seen in the distance once the forest began thinning out. Hanar trembled behind a large flowering bush. Talia put her hand on his shoulder. He jumped as if her hand were made of hot coals.

"You can't go any further. I will be all right from here. Just stay hidden and I will return as soon as I can."

Hanar grimaced and nodded. "They will have patrols out, so you won't get very close before they see you." His voice was shaky. "Be careful and whatever you do don't look at them straight in the eyes. They consider that a challenge, a sign of disrespect. The Centaurs are warriors and will take any excuse they're given to start a fight. It doesn't matter that you're a female. So be very careful."

"Don't worry," she said. "Everything will be fine. You'll see." She hugged him. "You just stay alert. I don't want to have to rescue you." She gave him a weak smile and headed out to cross the mile-wide clearing that surrounded the village.

Talia stepped with her head up, heading straight for the village.

She felt everything except confident. Her legs were wobbly, and she had to eventually look at her feet to keep from stumbling on the uneven ground. Talia couldn't figure out which fear was the greatest: the fear of being alone again, the fear of the Centaurs, the fear of not finding her mother and brother, or the fear of being rejected when she found them. Or even the fear of being so far away from the only place she had ever really known.

Lost in a maze of her dread and apprehension, looking down at her feet, Talia nearly impaled herself on the spear that was pointed at her chest. She looked up to see four grim-faced Centaurs surrounded her with angry looking weapons and angrier looking eyes. Talia remembered the warning Hanar had given her. Lowering her eyes, she stared at their chest.

"Hello," and a clumsy curtsy were all she could manage. Talia had only seen clay figures and paintings of Centaurs. Her father had told her stories and she had read tales of them, but the real things were much bigger and much scarier. Swallowing the lump of fear in her throat, she tried to keep her trembling legs from giving out. Talia had to fight to keep from turning and running back into the woods.

The Centaurs were muscular, barrel-chested, and hairy. Each one had his own unique markings tattooed on his body. She marveled at the impressive spiral horns and cloven ears of which hers were a sorry imitation. Thick beards and long coarse hair surrounded large intense eyes and wide-flaring nostrils. They looked like ferocious fighting men from the head to the waist, muscle bound and capable. From the waist down, they were majestic stallions. Their immense muscles seem to twitch with a desire to be tested and radiating a sense of power with every movement of a joint. A powerful equine torso of bulging tendons sat on hefty legs and hooved feet. A fine layer of silken hair bounced the light around their bodies accentuating the beautiful spectrum of colors. Solid or patterned, their coats gleamed like metal. A sense of power rippled through their finely-honed frames.

A particularly sour-faced Centaur with a large scar from his right cheek to his chin and his hair tied back with a rope prodded her with his spear. He pointed toward the village. They never spoke to her or each other, only gesturing in an unspoken language. Talia obeyed and moved forward escorted by the quartet. Hanar shivered behind the bush. His hands cupped his head, watching the scene and repeating over and over "Why did I let her go?"

As they approached the village, the inhabitants noticed their arrival and began to line the path into the village. The ground was hard and heavily trodden. Gritty dust flavored the air. Bare chested males and colorfully clad females of all ages and sizes lined the path, some with scowls, some with looks of surprise, but all staring curiously. Many excitedly whipped their tails, others cantered in place, and some stood firm with their arms crossed over their chest sternly appraising her.

Young children ran to their parents and peeked at the stranger from behind safe perches. Their large eyes had long waving black lashes as they blinked with wonder as if she were a newly discovered species. Muffled whispers and agitated grumblings echoed through the crowd.

Talia proceeded forward not knowing where she was going, afraid and unable to stop. She imagined walking straight through the village and escaping through the other side. The desire to see her mother and brother was the only thing holding her together.

The road was wide enough that her escorts could easily walk side by side as they pushed her further into the village. Rows of long rectangle wooden houses banded the road. At the corners of each house were stone pillars that held up the thatched roofs. Each house had a wide double door as an entrance, a stone chimney, and windows with wooden shutters. Large covered barrels for water sat near the entrance. Baskets full of fruits and vegetables hung from Sheppard's hooks along the side of the houses. There were wide spaces between each house that led to other roads. Talia wondered how large the village really was. There were at least two trees around every house. It was as if they had brought the forest into the village.

Flowers and bushes sprung up all over, making the trails a colorful thoroughfare within the village. The whole place was awash in color.

Not only the land, but also the inhabitants were arrayed in bright cheerful patterns. The mixture of nature, utility, and artistry surprised her. She would have thought that a warrior race would distain art and beauty, not embrace it in such a personal way. She expected a dull colorless scene full of drab colors with cold steel and hard edges: a place of stone and metal. But the homes were full of vitality, displaying the beauty and warmth of the nature around them.

There was a strong smell of spices in the air, hints of rosemary, cumin, peppercorn, and sage. Outdoor pits smoked with the aroma of braising meats. Kettles steamed and bubbled with the promise of spicy dishes. She saw through the spaces between the houses, corrals holding sheep and goats, coops with chickens, and pens for pigs. Quails and pheasants, freshly slaughtered, hung from lines stretched between poles. Each house had a small garden sprouting fresh vegetables and herbs.

However, the vestments of war were there as well. There were stands of fighting poles, swords, and spears. Posts holding bows and quills stood between every house. Elaborately adorned armor breast plates, helmets, shields, and leg guards were laid out on tables before each dwelling, cleaned and polished, gleaming like precious stones, easily accessible and ready to be yielded.

The sound of grunts and shouts drew her attention as pairs of Centaurs with fight poles and swords exercised in a field off to one side. They stopped and stared as the procession passed by. There were stacks of hay with targets painted on them and arrows stuck in them displaying deadly accuracy. Off in the distance, Talia heard the familiar "clang, clang" of a blacksmith's hammer striking an anvil. It made her think of Barnabus and his dire warnings. She wondered if she should have listened and stayed away from here. *I hope you were wrong, Barnabus.* She thought.

Talia studied every face; looking for one that fit the description her father had given her. She remembered it word for word. As a child, she would often lay in her bed and try to paint the face she held in her mind.

"She was beautiful," Talleon would say. "She had almond shaped eyes that were the azure blue of a cloudless summer sky. Her skin was a creamy chestnut color, it looked and felt like Aldarren silk. Her black silky hair was braided and twisted in a crown that sat between her small white spiral horns. She had a small defiant nose. Her full red lips looked like they were ready to laugh, and her voice always sounded as if it was about to break out in song."

Whenever he described her, he smiled and stared into space as if the remembering transported him back to her. His words never changed, and she cherished every time he spoke them. Talia studied every face looking for the mother she longed to know.

The march stopped in front of a small round windowless building separated from the others and visible on all sides. One of the Centaurs opened the door and pushed her in. No one had spoken a word to her or given any indication of her fate. Once she was locked away, Talia heard whispering and laughter outside. The constant "clip-clop" of marching hoofs was a reminder of who her captors were and how tenuous her situation was. Talia sat on the only thing in the room, a bale of straw. For what seemed like hours, no one came. She banged on the door and called out.

"Someone, please. Can I talk to someone?" The door swung open. The Centaur with the long facial scar glared in at her, leveling his spear. He flared his nostrils and slammed the door shut again.

With the approaching evening, the door sprang open. A Centaur clad in a white vestment and large gold medallion dangling around his neck burst into the room. He rushed in like a flash of lightning. A mane of white hair flowed over his shoulders. He was aged, but as physically intimidating as the others. His eyes screamed long before he used his voice. He was assessing her with a stare of iron. The booming voice caused her to lose her breath; the sound bombarded her like ice pellets in a hailstorm. Talia backed away against the wall. She would have fallen to the ground if not for the support the wall provided.

"I am Marreanus, leader of the Centaurs," he declared proudly. "Who are you, and why have you dared to trespass on Centaur land?" It sounded more like a decree than a question.

Regaining her balance, she answered with as much courage as she could muster. "I am Talia, daughter of the great Sorcerer Talleon of Mandoria. I have come in search of..." She hesitated. Doubt over took her, not sure if she should reveal her true mission. *What if revealing my real reason will put me in jeopardy. Or my mother and brother? What if my origin could be offensive to them? What if...*

He interrupted her thoughts "In search of what?" he demanded.

"I am a Sorceress. I seek wisdom. I've come to learn from your wise Shaman. I have heard the magic of the Centaurs is powerful and true." She tried not to show the discomfort that lying caused her by stiffening her legs and standing as straight and as tall as she could.

"Humans are not permitted to experience our ways. Sorceress or not, you have broken our laws and must be judged and punished."

"Even those that share a kinship with you?"

"A kinship?" He repeated with a grin. "What kinship could you have with Centaurs?" A laugh sat on his lips.

Talia threw off her cloak, gathered her hair back in a tail to reveal her Centaur ears and parted her locks to reveal her horn buds.

"Even one that shares the noble blood of the Centaurs? One who comes freely and openly among you without treachery or deception?"

Marreanus' eyes grew wide. He reared up almost touching the ceiling. "How is this possible? You are Human, not Centaur. This must be some of your wicked magic."

"I am of the blood. It is no trick. If you do not believe me have your Shaman test me. I will not resist."

"This I will do. We will know the truth of things." He snorted. "And if we find out that this is some Human trick, the price you pay will be two-fold."

He bellowed like a Dragon, turned, and trotted out the door, slamming the door with a kick of his hind legs. The building shook from the effort.

Talia sat and released the breath she had been holding. *I know I lied to Marreanus, but it will give me time to figure out what to do. Maybe after the Shaman confirms that I'm part Centaur, I will be able to find my mother and brother. Once they're found everything will be better. They will help.* She was sure of it; at least she hoped so. Her thoughts moved to Hanar. She knew he had seen them take her into the village. Talia hoped he was safe and well hidden. *How long will he wait for me? Would he do something crazy like come into the village and try to rescue me?* She hoped he wouldn't. He seemed to feel a certain responsibility for her that might cause him to do something stupid. "No, Hanar," she whispered. "Go home. This is beyond you now. Be safe." Her worry for her new friend helped her calm her fears about her own troubles.

CHAPTER 7

The Centaurs' Shaman entering her prison the next morning awakened Talia, who was wrapped in her cloak. Two guards with swords drawn, ready to defend her accompanied the Shaman, who was short and thin. Talia could feel the power radiating from her. She walked in with her guard up and her magic ready to spring. The old Centaur had stringy gray hair that hung freely and swayed as she made her slow movements into the room. She proceeded with a measured gait and used a shortened elaborately carved fighting pole as a cane. The same shapes and symbols that were drawn on her arms and legs were also etched onto the staff. She wore a bodice made of sun-bleached clamshells and an amulet of lapis lazuli. Her large gray eyes were clear and alert like a hawk's and moved about the room searching for any danger.

Talia stood, bowed from the waist, and remained silent.

Without speaking, the Shaman came to Talia, lifted her hair with wiry fingers and examined her ears and her horn buds. Talia did not resist. She placed her palm to Talia's forehead, closed her eyes, and mumbled in a language Talia didn't recognize.

"Hmm," she grunted looking Talia over from head to toe. "What would you do with a mixture of Yoba roots, tannor berries, and swamp fly buds?"

'Nothing," said Talia in a solemn tone. "That would kill you. If you substitute the tannor berries with knuckle root sprouts, you could use it as a poultice to cure rashes."

'Creyon powder?"

'Morning sickness for those with child."

'Ashberries?"

'In a tea to calm the heart or as a salve to soothe a wound."

The old woman held out her hand. A small blue ball of light appeared and floated inches above her palm. "Take it."

Talia opened her hand and said, "Come here, little one." The globe drifted to her out-stretched palm, doubled in size and turned white. She smiled at the old woman. "This," she said, "is like the games my father and I used to play when I was younger. It was his way to see if I was progressing in my studies." She snapped the fingers on her other hand and the globe disappeared. "It was one of the best parts of my lessons."

'Yes, your father taught you well," responded the old Centaur, smiling and shaking her head. She looked to the guards and motioned for them to leave. After they left and the door was closed, she turned to Talia and asked:

'Why are you really here? You have not come to learn what you already know. I have no doubt that I may be able to teach you a trick or two, but that is not why you are here. Is it?" Talia's face flushed. The old Centaur tilted her head and narrowed her eyes.

'Is it to discover your other half, perhaps? To learn who and why you are, or do you already know that much?" She was making a statement more than asking a question, with a knowing bob of her head.

Talia reddened with the embarrassment of discovery. "I am sorry that I lied to Marreanus, but I wasn't sure that he would understand or accept my claim."

'As one conjuror to another, I must say that you were wise in your hesitation. If it was discovered that one of our Mares coupled with a Human she would be ridiculed and exiled at best, killed at worst." The

Shaman paused and shook her head. "I do not believe in accidents. I have lived long enough to know that the gods do things for a reason. Why you were born and why you are here now mean something. Something not only for you but something for us. The Centaur clan is going through some major changes. We will soon leave this land. What you may have to do with that has yet to be discovered."

She raised her chin and spoke like a general commanding his troops. "What is your name, child?"

"I am Talia."

"Talia? Oh really...interesting." A questioning look crossed her face. She looked at Talia more intensely as if recognition came to her, but quickly brushed it aside. "I am Ladena." The old Shaman studied her for a few moments. "Do you have the sight yet?"

"Only in rare flashes," Talia said. "When I find myself entering scary moments, I sometimes get brief images."

"That is to be expected. The sight comes mostly with age and experience. You are still very young. In time, and with practice it will come to you, I'm sure. One day you may be able to call upon it and even control it. Magic, like most things in life, is not easy, despite any natural tendencies you have for it. You cannot force that which will not and cannot be rushed. Come," she ordered leading the way out of the door.

As they walked down the center of the village, Talia couldn't help but feel probing eyes studying her every move. Eyes were peeking out of windows, around corners, and behind trees. She wondered if a pair of those eyes belonged to her mother or to her brother. As they walked to the edge of the village, Talia was aware of the corner-of-the-eye stare the Shaman was giving her. The old Shaman was still assessing and studying her and gauging her reactions. *Earning her trust,* Talia thought, *"will not be so easy."*

Ladena's house was the last one in the village. It sat on the far east border of the settlement next to a cemetery. Dozens and dozens of gravestones dotted the landscape. Talia took on an expression of surprise as she surveyed the graveyard.

"I prefer the company of the departed." Ladena said, noticing her surprise. "They are quieter and less complicated." She smiled.

"Let's get you settled in before I go speak to Marreanus about you. Then we shall sit down, and you can tell me your story. The whole story." The old shaman raised her brows to emphasize the words.

CHAPTER 8

*L*adena's house was a square box and half the size of the other homes. It was blanketed with flowers of all sizes and shapes. Purple and red vines bejeweled with large vibrant blooms made a path to the front door. The house looked like it had been grown instead of built. The flowers and vines clung to the walls like icing on a cake. The stunning colors were a delight to the eyes. Sunshine shimmered off the petals like light reflecting off beveled mirrors. The air was alive with intoxicating fragrances that made you want to breathe in, over and over again. The large exotic blossoms climbed to the roof and cascaded back down splashing in a waterfall of colors that framed the house with a velvety border.

Flamboyantly colored butterflies, moths, and iridescent humming-birds flitted about sating themselves on sweet sticky nectars. The butterflies played games of tag as they flittered from bloom to bloom, sampling the sweet essence. Jewel-chested humming birds zipped back and forth like shooting stars, stabbing their delicate beaks in pools of nectars before darting off to another delight. Frenzied yellow and black striped bees hopped from flower to flower diving deep into floral pools, emerging covered in powdery flakes of pollen like children in a sand box.

"I have never seen such beautiful flowers. Your home is lovely."

"I am glad you like it. I have a special fondness for blossoms. They are an indulgence. Their colors and fragrances renew my spirit. They remind me of the beauty and plenty of life."

"Oh yes. I love it. It's like living inside a flower garden." Ladena smiled and nodded at the comparison.

Inside the house there were runes painted on the walls, ceiling, and floor. Artifacts, relics, and charms made of bones, colored stones, and flattened metal discs hung on the walls and dangled from the ceiling. The large table that dominated the room was laden with bowls, jars, and half completed potions. Shelves full of containers with a collection of herbs and spices covered an entire wall. Bunches of plants tied to ropes hung drying, suspended from the rafters. A three-legged stool, a stone fireplace with a stone mantel, and hearth completed the room.

Talia smiled at the familiar scents that assaulted her nose and took her back to her father's workroom. Her senses tingled at the familiar and were excited by the new and unknown. Feeling as though she was in a place she could relate to helped Talia to relax. Magic lived here, and that made it feel safe and right.

Ladena made her some Bramberry tea, a plate of roasted pork, leafy greens, and sourdough bread.

"Eat child," she said. "You will need your strength. I see much ahead for us." The look she gave Talia was both curious and concerning. Ladena departed, leaving Talia to eat and consider her next move.

After Talia ate, she stepped outside to look around. Looking toward the forest, she hoped in one way that Hanar had left and returned home. In another way, she hoped that he was still waiting for her. If she knew he was still out there, she wouldn't feel so alone. Scanning the forest around the village there was no sign nor signal from him. Talia remembered the flute and decided she might try it out later that night when things quieted down. Hopefully, no one would see her or Hanar.

*L*ocated in the center of the village, the meeting hall was twice the size of the other buildings in the community. The other houses fanned out from it like the arms of a giant beast. Ladena entered, raised her cane, and slammed it onto the wooden floor causing a thunderous echo. All heads in the room looked her way. Only one member of the group interested her. "Marreanus we must speak," she said demanding his attention.

"Just a moment, Ladena," he said dismissively over his shoulder not bothering to face her.

"Now," she demanded raising her voice as if talking to a disobedient child.

He hesitated, spun to look at her, and then signaled for the room to be cleared. Imposing-looking male figures scurried cautiously around Ladena, giving her a wide berth, each well aware of the power the small, wrinkled figure wielded.

"What is the need for these dramas Ladena? Your outbursts..."

"It has begun," she interrupted. "I warned you some time ago that this day was coming. This child is the beginning. She is an opening, a start. She is surely part of us. Her mother, whoever she is or was, came from here, our clan. Her coming was inevitable and unavoidable. It surely will bring about a great change. Either we will embrace this change or be destroyed. It is time we prepare for the return."

"How can this abomination be a sign? Be a part of us?"

"Huh. Such a small mind." She wagged her head. "Are you standing so firmly in the past that you cannot see the future before you? She is not an abomination. She is a sign of our future if we remain here. A reminder of what we left in the past."

Ladena smacked her lips and shook her head. "I told you and all the council some time ago that forces were aligning. Maybe for us; maybe against us. I cannot be certain. I warned you we would face a challenge that will alter us forever. She is only a glimpse of that test. There is much more to uncover. The signs do not lie, Marreanus. These will be our last days if we remain here. Staying will make us be not what we should be, but something other than we are." She leaned on her cane and stared into the distance. Her words seeming to draw the vitality from her like the melting away of snow.

"This place we have been forced into is not our own. It is not of us or for us. We have stayed as long as we dare. It is rejecting us. We water the land with the blood of our warriors and receive no yield. More of us die and less of us are born. We have no future here. It is time to return to the soil of our birth. To return to the source. To leave while we still have a legacy to pass on. To return home. Our penance has been paid. We have earned back our place." She raised weary eyes to meet his.

"I don't know if I can survive this. Though I long for home and know we must return, my life force, my family's blood has been spent here. Home cries out to me, but so much of me is here. Buried up in this soil. I no longer feel the loss that drove us from our home. So much has transpired since then. I only feel the pull of the souls we have planted here."

She slammed her staff down as if she were injecting her pain into the floor, passing it from herself into the building. The sound lingered through the hall like a dying wail.

"Ladena," Marreanus started, his brow arching over his eyes like an umbrella. "I long to return home, but I do not like the idea of leaving like this. We are under attack. It seems as if we are retreating, running in fear. We are warriors. Warriors do not retreat. Warriors do not run."

"Marreanus!" She shouted pulling her face into a tight ball of wrinkles.

"I know," he sighed. "I hoped things would change, but..."

"As did I," she agreed.

"Reports on the Wolfmen." He waved a hefty scroll. "Their movements, their numbers and possible intentions. Before we depart we may have a war to settle. The Wolves are irrepressible. Then there are the Humans." He spit the word out. "Digging for gold and silver like badgers hunting for roots. We have chased them from the eastern hills too many times. They are more a nuisance than a threat, but their presence taxes us. They have offered no real resistance but sooner or later they will. Ladena, we are surrounded by adversaries and you want me to worry about prophesies and omens?"

Sitting down on a bench as if the question was too heavy to hold up, Marreanus closed his eyes and massaged his brow. His voice trickled out slow and somber. "Surrendering what has been so hard fought to obtain? I know we must leave these lands, but we will not be chased away like rabbits. My heart does not know how to surrender."

Marreanus searched the floor looking for a lost thought. "I see how the fire has dwindled in some of the young. I know we are not what we used to be."

Ladena smiled. "Yes, I know your warrior's heart aches at this. The Wolves are a threat, a serious adversary. Since the first day of our arrival, they have been an obstacle to our survival. The Humans, in time, will be an even greater one. We and the Wolves will fade from this land. There is little magic left in it. This is a place for men and their reason. Not creatures of legend, creatures of magic, like us. We have and always will have those who drive us to war it is part of who we are. Part of what we do. But, don't lose sight of what is most important. Do you not understand that what we do about this could mean whether we fade from history or live to make it? Just remember that your decisions and actions not only affect what happens now, but also determine if there will be a tomorrow for us at all.

"Don't dismiss this. Don't confuse what is worth fighting for with pride. Forces are gathering, lines are converging, and the powers beyond us are calling our name. It will soon be our time to act or be acted upon. The question is, do we live, or do we die."

Ladena rested both hands on her staff, leaned toward Marreanus and smiled. Cocking her head and winking one eye she motioned upward with a cackle. "That crown you fought so hard to claim grows quite heavy. Does it not?"

He glared at her out of the corner of his eyes but did not reply.

"As for the child," she straightened up. "I will deal with her and try to learn what I can. She is no danger. I am sure of it. As a matter of fact, I rather like her. To have the courage to walk into our midst, alone, unarmed, and subject herself to our whims. Besides, who knows, she may very well turn out to be useful." She turned and walked away with the confidence gait of age.

CHAPTER 9

When Ladena returned to the house, Talia had washed herself, her clothes, and the dishes. Her garments hung drying on a post behind the house. She was sitting on a stool wrapped in her cloak.

"I see that you have made yourself at home."

"I hope you don't mind. I was so dirty. I haven't been able to wash in days and..."

"No, no child. I'm glad you took it upon yourself. I am sorry I have no clothing to offer you. Now," she said groaning as she lowered herself down on her haunches, her hands resting on the pole planted firmly in front of her. "How do you come to be here?"

Talia moved the stool next to her. "I was raised by my father in Mandoria. He..."

"Talia," she blurted out. "Your beginning is where you must start. Who, child, is your mother? When and where did she meet your father?"

Talia hesitated. Her clear emerald eyes became cloudy like grass wet with dew. She buried her face in her hands and began to weep. Talia did not realize how much tension and anxiety she was holding in. The thoughts of her mother and brother broke in on her and all the pain flowed out of her on the backs of large abundant tears.

Ladena let her cry. "Let it all out. I have the feeling that you have been carrying much too much for far too long."

When the tears exhausted themselves, Talia looked up into Ladena's face and saw tears zigzagging down the wrinkled folds of her wrinkled face. "Ladena?" she whispered, puzzled at her reaction. Ladena reached her withered fingers out and touched the amulet that had exposed itself as the top of Talia's cloak had fallen open.

"Cyrenia was your mother," she moaned. Her voice was thin and almost a sigh.

"Yes," she answered. "But, how did you know?"

"I should have known." She pounded her leg. "I should have seen it, felt it. How could I be so blind?" The old Shaman wiped her eyes and continued. "Because, you wear the amulet given to her by her mother. By me."

"You, her mother. But..."

"Let me tell you a story." Ladena said softly batting her eyes to slow the flow of tears.

"Twenty summers ago, shortly after we arrived here, there was a great battle between the Wolfmen and the Centaurs. It was inevitable. We are too different and yet too alike to share a land. Our two clans had been at odds from our first encounter. The fighting was fierce and brutal. It is known as the Battle for Glory. We were victorious, but many great warriors died that day. My mate, Mallas, and my brother, Vardus, were two of the casualties. I thought Cyrenia had died too. A noble death for a Centaur, but still hard for a mother to take. That day I lost my whole family: my child, my mate, and my brother.

"Later when we searched the battlefield for our dead, to bring them home for burial, Cyrenia's body could not be found. I went mad with grief. We thought that the Wolfmen had taken and eaten her since they do not take captives. I nearly died from the pain. I mourned for months and months. Then one day, a little over a year later Cyrenia returned. She had a child, a boy, your brother Cyron, with her. She would not tell us where she had been only that she had been badly wounded and nursed back to health. I could see the humanity in the boy, but I never spoke of it. I was just so happy to have my Cyrenia back. I did not press the matter."

Ladena continued to weep as she stroked Talia's hair. "I should have known." She cupped Talia's face. "I don't know why I didn't see it before. You have your mother's countenance, her strength."

"Where is my mother? I want to meet her. I have dreamt of her all my life."

The flow of tears increased. "I am sorry my child. Your mother died last winter. She was out with a patrol. There was an ambush. They were all killed."

Talia froze as if she had just walked upon some sudden horror. The whole world flipped upside down. She felt as if she had just been told that the sky was really the ground and she was walking on air. Nothing made sense. She did not cry as much as she sweated tears. It felt as if ever part of her body was melting away. Talia and Ladena fell into each other and wept like stormy clouds.

Ladena pulled herself to her feet with the help of the pole. She took Talia's hand in hers and led her silently down the path to the cemetery. There they found the stone marking the grave of the mother she would never get to meet. Talia sank down in front of the grave and stared at the stone. She hugged her cloak tight around herself. Ladena turned back to the house and left them to get acquainted.

Hours later, looking worn and haggard, Talia returned to the house. Her eyes were the color of beets, her voice hoarse and wispy. She held her trembling chin up. Sitting beside Ladena she took her hands. "You and Cyron are my only family now. If you will have me..."

"Have you, child?" She pulled her into an embrace. "I cherish you. I knew your coming was something special. You are my daughter returned to me. You are a blessing from the Gods."

"Do you think Cyron will accept me?"

"Cyron does not know about you as I did not know. It will be a shock to him. But, his heart is large, there is room for you."

"Cyrenia never said anything about his father?" Anger began to mix with grief and she wasn't sure which to feel. "My father loved her. He told me all about her. He talked about her all the time."

Ladena tilted her head giving a skeptical look. "Be honest now. Did he really tell you all about her? Did he really talk about her all the time?"

'Yes, well no." She reluctantly admitted. "He rarely talked about her. I had to beg him to get the little I learned over the years. But..."

'That's right. Don't judge them. They knew they could never truly be together. Each had to carve out their own lives. I believe Cyrenia thought the two of them would never meet again. As well, that she would never see you again. She had to know that Cyron would have a hard enough time and did not want to burden him with things he could not change." She paused and chuckled. "You have the ears and horns he has been looking for all his life. He may be a bit jealous of that."

"Where is he?"

"He is away on patrol now, but he will be returning soon. It will give us time alone to get to know each other better."

Ladena and Talia spent the rest of the evening and well into the night talking. Ladena told her about her mother and the Centaurs. Talia introduced Ladena to her father, Thangor, the goings on at the castle, and Hanar. Talia avoided conversation about Cyron. She wanted to meet him for herself.

CHAPTER 10

The band of young Centaurs progressed restlessly through the early morning light toward the village. Smoke from the chimneys could be seen just past the tree line. Away from the comfort of home for several weeks, they were anxious to return. During their patrol of the borders, they had battled with Wolfmen and driven off gangs of Human miners in the foothills. Most important was the alarming news that the Wolfmen and the Humans were forming alliances. A Wolfman had been captured who had a message scroll from Phalon, leader of the Wolfmen, to the royal court in Mandoria. "Marreanus will be pleased with this valuable piece of information," Tyrel said, waving the scroll.

"Yes," answered Cyron. "Maybe we'll be rewarded with new breast plates or shields, even though I would prefer a new bow and quills."

"You're already the best archer in the clan, Cyron. What do you need with another bow? You win every archery contest. Give the rest of us a chance," protested Tyrel.

"Breast plates and shields" another young Centaur seconded.

"More likely," said Tyrel. "he'll figure out a way to take the credit for himself and forget about us."

"Don't be so hard on Marreanus. His is a difficult job. I would think that you would be more supportive of your father," Cyron countered.

"I am. I do, but just because he's my father doesn't mean I can't disagree with him. Who's been off tracking through the woods for the last few weeks? Eating whatever we could hunt down; sleeping out in the open, away from our kin and women folk, not to mention fighting Wolves and Humans. All he does is give speeches all day." Tyrel said.

"He's got a point," was the response.

"Marreanus was once a great warrior. He fought in many great battles. He uses his wisdom instead of his sword these days. Maybe one day Tyrel, when you are the leader of the clan and your fighting days have passed, you may not see things the same way you do now." said Cyron.

"Of course not. That's why I complain now. Later I'll sit around and blame everything on you." They all laughed.

Cyron was different from the other young Centaurs. He was shorter and not as burly. Still his muscles were lean and well defined. Instead of the growing beard and hairy chest of the others, his body was smooth and hairless. He grew his thick black hair longer than most, and let it hang loose in an attempt to hide his Human-shaped ears and other attributes. While the others boasted and showed off their growing horns, Cyron's lack of horns once again reminded everyone that he was different. He compensated for his differences by being the best young warrior in the village and by excelling in every area. No one was braver, shot an arrow straighter, or fought with more passion than he.

'Go ahead without me," Cyron said to the group. "I want to check Mansa's traps. It'll save the old war horse the trouble of coming out here."

'Don't take too long or you'll miss the celebration." yelled Tyrel as the group continued to march away.

'I won't," yelled Cyron "'I'll be right behind you." After the group had moved out of sight, Cyron took his bow from his shoulder and withdrew a quill from the pouch on his back. He loaded the bow, turned and pointed it at a tall thicket of corn grass. He was erect as a tree, holding the tension tight on his bow.

"I don't know who you are, but I've got a solid aim on you. Come out or I'll send this arrow in to find you."

He paused. "I won't ask again". His finger was itching to release the quill.

The grass ruffled and a curly headed Satyr with his arms raised emerged. "Don't shoot. I don't mean any harm."

"Who are you? Why have you been following us all morning? Spying for the accursed Wolves, I'd say."

"I would never do anything like that," he said, contempt in his voice. "I hate them. They killed my parents."

"Then why didn't you make your presence known. Are you a thief?"

"No, I'm no thief. I didn't want to be captured and made a slave or a pet."

"What are you talking about?"

"My father said that Centaurs make us their slaves and pets."

"We don't have slaves and as for a pet, I don't think you'd be very entertaining." He laughed. "Besides, that's an old tale made up to scare children. Are you a child?"

"I'm almost 18 seasons old," the Satyr said, puffing out his slim chest."

Cyron released the tension and lowered his bow. "What do you want little Satyr?"

Swallowing the indignity, he said. "My name is Hanar, Hanar Knoll. I heard them call you Cyron and I was worried about your sister."

"I don't have a sister."

"Yes, you do," he said, smiling and eager to tell what he knew. "Her name is Talia and she's at the village right now. I know because I took her there. I haven't seen or heard from her since they took her prisoner. I wanted to ask you to help."

Cyron laughed. "You have the wrong Centaur. If I had a sister I would know it. Since I don't, you are wrong." Cyron wagged a finger at him. "Don't follow me again. Next time I might shoot first." He turned and started to trot away.

"Wait," Hanar said chasing after him. "Your sister Talia is a Human and the Centaurs may hurt..."

Before he could finish his statement Cyron had turned, charged at him and was holding him up by his throat. "I don't know what game you're playing, but I don't like it."

Hanar was struggling against the iron grip that held him suspended in midair. "She...ears...horns," was all he could manage to get out before Cyron flung him into a nearby tree.

"I should flay you alive," Cyron said standing over him with his sword drawn and raised, his green eyes on fire with rage and his chest rising and falling like a bellows.

"To say such things is an insult to me and my family. Don't ever say such a thing again." He pointed his sword directly in the prostate Satyr's face. "Stay away from me or you'll regret it."

Over matched, Hanar remained silent. Full of anger and fury, Cyron flared his nostrils and galloped away toward the village.

When he reached the village, Cyron's boil had lessened to a simmer. Still unsettled by his encounter in the woods, he chose to go home instead of seeking out the others and joining in the return home celebration. The words, ears, and horns picked at his mind like pins being jabbed into his skull.

All the pain of being different rushed at him. Cyron remembered the constant teasing and taunting he endured as a child because of his Human ears and lack of horns. He remembered how the others said he wasn't a real Centaur and how he was less than them. He also remembered the way they dismissed him and refused to allow him to play or train with them, the way he had to work twice as hard as the others to become an accepted part of the clan even though he was as strong and clever as anyone. No matter what he did, he had to prove himself over and over again.

The rejection and unhappiness that plagued his childhood left deep wounds. The Satyr's mention of his ears and horns was like picking at a sore that hadn't healed yet. It was still raw and tender.

Cyron felt as if the Satyr had grabbed that scab and yanked it off. His mother's and grandmother's words of sympathy and encouragement had never been enough. Their assurances didn't ease his need to belong and be accepted.

As his anger revved up again and promised to explode, there was a knock at the door. Racing to the door, his nostrils pumping like engines and his eyes burning embers of fire, he flung the door open and nearly trampled his young visitor.

"What do you want?" He shouted causing the adolescent Centaur to rear back in fright.

Wide eyed with fear, the youngster stuttered "La...Ladena sent me to tell you to come to her. She said to come now..." he turned and raced away.

Cyron watched the young one speeding away and felt regret for his lack of control. He saw the ghost of his past self in the frightened face of the young one and felt a twinge of shame for his behavior. He would have to make it up to him later. Closing the door, he headed to Ladena's.

CHAPTER 11

*W*hen Cyron entered the house, Ladena was leaning over a bowl mixing one of the many potions he had watched her make while growing up. She looked up from her work and saw the expression of anger in his eyes, a look he wore all through his childhood.

Lowering her head and tendering to her mixing, she asked. "What has angered you Cyron?" Before he could open his mouth to deny his anger she added. "I am as familiar with your anger and your temper as you are, so do not deny it."

Feeling like the pie thief caught with the evidence on his face, he bent his head. "In the woods coming home a Satyr was following us. He angered me with wild stories and I..."

"You *what?*" Came an excited voice. Cyron turned around to see a lovely young woman with emerald eyes staring intently at him. A Human woman. "You *what?*" She asked again. "You didn't hurt him, did you?"

"I might have a little." He mumbled tilting his head. "Who are you?" He blurted out.

"Oh no, Hanar!" she shouted. Her face went pale with worry.

"Where did you leave him?" When he didn't immediately answer, she shouted, her hands clenched in fists. "Where?"

"Just west of the village." He pointed weakly, unsure of how to respond.

"If you've hurt him," she threatened, grabbing her cloak and running for the door.

He turned to his grandmother. "Ladena?" A look of astonishment was on his face.

"Go with her. Help her," said Ladena, a small smile at the corner of her mouth. She raised her eyes to him and added. "Oh yes, say hello to your sister."

Cyron stood transfixed and unable to complete a thought. He looked from Ladena to the open door and back again. He laughed. "My sister, but..." The question froze on his lips. His legs involuntary began cantering in place.

"Yes," Ladena pointed toward the door, never looking up from her bowl and pestle. "This should come as a pleasant surprise to you, her name is Talia."

"Talia? Talia...but?" His head swung back and forth from the door to Ladena and back again. "Talia?"

"Yes," she nodded. "Answers some questions, doesn't it?" She smiled and pointed to the door, again. "Now go."

His mouth moved as if he was speaking, but no words came out. Turning to the door he took off after the angry young woman.

Talia raced through the village dodging carts and groups of romping children. She flew through the market square, not paying any attention to the crowds of busy shoppers. Talia plowed through a flock of chickens, sending them scattering in all directions. She bumped a table of melons, causing them to roll across the road, sending cursing merchants chasing the escaping produce. She paid no heed to the glares and disapproving stares that blocked her path. Everyone in the village had been told of her arrival, and they openly expressed their disapproval or their indifference. The shouts and curses thrown at her did not affect her pace. She single-mindedly pursued her goal until she reached the edge of the village. Cyron caught up with her as she passed the last building at the edge of the village.

She looked at him a tight-lipped frown on her face. Scanning left to right. She asked. "Where?" He pointed to her left and she was off again. A patrol of four Centaurs saw them and began approaching. Cyron waved them off and continued to pursue her. When she reached the tree line she began calling.

"Hanar, Hanar. Where are you? It's Talia..." Cyron was close behind her.

"I left him over there," he pointed to the tree near the thicket of corn grass where he first saw Hanar. "He was resting against that tree when I left." He said innocently.

"Resting?" She said her tone telling him she did not believe his description. She went to the tree and saw the smear of blood against the bark. Rubbing her fingers in the liquid she turned her red stained hand to Cyron.

"How could you? He's harmless. There's no way you could have felt threatened."

Before he could answer she dashed away shouting, "Hanar, Hanar. It's Talia. Where are you? Please be all right." Cyron trailed behind her not knowing how to explain. She finally collapsed on a stump sobbing.

"He's all right. He's just hiding somewhere," offered Cyron.

She looked up at him and said, "Stay away from me and don't speak to me. You probably killed him. He's probably somewhere dying." Talia remembered the flute and stood taking it from the pocket of her cloak. Frantically she blew into it between sobs, blowing until she was out of breath and collapsed back on the stump in tears.

"I'm sorry," he said approaching her. "Are you really my sister?"

She looked up at him with irritation in her eyes. "Don't remind me."

"I didn't ask for a sister. Especially a Human one," he snapped back.

She stood and confronted him. "I didn't ask for a brute for a brother, either. As a matter of fact, you can..."

"Talia."

She stopped cold. "Hanar. Is that you?" she shouted.

"Yes. It's me."

"Are you all right? Where are you?"

"I'm not coming out with him there."

Cyron pointed to a large oak choked with purple vines. Talia rushed to the tree. "Come on out Hanar. It's safe. He won't harm you. Will you?" She said turning and frowning at Cyron.

"No," Cyron offered shaking his head. She jerked her head prodding him on. "I'm sorry if I hurt you," he said kicking the ground around him.

A furry hoofed leg inched from behind the tree and Hanar stepped out to reveal himself, bruised, but intact. Talia ran to him and hugged him. "I was so worried. Are you hurt badly?"

"I'll be all right. Just keep him away from me," pointing at Cyron.

"Don't worry about him. That's the last time that will ever happen. Isn't it?" she demanded. Cyron shook his head yes. "Let's get you fixed up. Where are you living?"

"I've found a hollow inside a grove of maples. It's not far."

Hanar and Talia walked side by side, she was holding him up like a child learning to walk. Cyron followed in silence. Talia scowled at Cyron.

"We'll need water. I assume you can do that without attacking anyone."

Cyron stamped off in the direction of a nearby stream mumbling about his innocence. When he returned, having knitted together some large collop leaves to make a small basket, he spilled half of the water by slamming it down in front of her. She ignored him. Talia had searched the area and found some herbs to make a poultice for his wounds. She skillfully grounded them with a stone, added some of the water, and began tending to his wounds.

"I was very worried about you. I watched the patrol take you into the village. I," Hanar hung his head in shame. "I was too afraid to come into the village. There are so many of them and they're so big." He looked at Cyron. "I was going to ask him for help, but he..."

Cyron hunched his shoulders and said, "I didn't know."

"It's alright, Hanar. I found what I was looking for. My mother," she swallowed and looked to Cyron. "Our mother is dead. I'll never get the chance to meet her. But, I did meet my grandmother. She is like me. She's the village Shaman."

"You're a Shaman?" asked an amazed Cyron.

"I'm a Sorceress like my...like our father. When I get over being angry at you, if I ever do, I may," she emphasized the words. "tell you something about him."

"And I can tell you all about...uhh...our mother," he added gleefully. For the first time, they shared a smile.

"I'm sorry about your mother." said Hanar, standing and rubbing his stomach. "You can stop fussing over me. I'm all right and I'm hungry. Let's eat. The pickings are a little scarce around here. It's not like at home, but I can gather enough for us to have a nice meal."

"Let me," offered Cyron. "I know the best fruit trees and where there are some rabbit traps close by. I'll be back soon. Make a fire," he yelled as he trotted away.

"I'm glad you're all right," said Hanar. "I was so worried. Tell me everything that happened." Talia relayed her adventures of the last couple of days as Hanar stared with his mouth hanging open in delight.

Cyron returned with an arm full of berries and fruits. He skinned and skewered the two rabbits from Mansa's traps and set them to roasting. He would make it up to Mansa later. They cooked and talked as the afternoon passed and dusk began to descend. The tension of the day began ebbing away and laughter began to enter the conversation.

"It's getting late," said Hanar. "You should probably get back to the village."

"I'm not leaving you alone tonight," Talia said.

"I'm fine. You don't have to worry about me."

"I'm staying," she insisted crossing her arms.

"Is she always like this?" Asked Cyron.

"Ever since I've known her," answered Hanar, shrugging his shoulders.

"I'm not all that surprised. The females in my family seem to be like that. It takes a little getting used to, but you soon learn to live with it," Cyron answered, tossing up a berry and catching it in his mouth.

"Don't talk about me like I'm not here," Talia said, looking from one to the other. They burst out in laughter. The trio spent the rest of the evening and late into the night eating, sharing stories, laughing, and getting to know each other.

CHAPTER 12

*H*anar retreated to the hollow in the tree to sleep and recover, leaving Talia and Cyron alone. The awkwardness of being strangers returned to their conversation. It forced them to face a past they shared but had not spent together.

"Why are you staring at me?"

Cyron shrugged his shoulders. "I'm just trying to see if we look like brother and sister. I mean, I look like a Centaur and you look like a Human. How can we be brother and sister?"

"I don't know it just the way the magic divided between us. We each got a piece of Cyrenia and Talleon. And a piece of each other. We're the joining of two worlds." She stood posing with her arm crossed before her. "Do I look like Cyrenia? Am I my mother's daughter?"

"Yes. I see her in you. You have her nose and complexion. I hear the same music in your voice. When she talked, it was like she was about to sing. You also have that same sad expression in your eyes as if you're carrying some great burden."

"That's funny. Father said the same thing about her voice, but not the thing about being sad."

"What about me? Do I look anything like Talleon?" Cyron asked, raising his chin in a noble pose.

"Of course, you do. When I first saw you, I was surprised how much like Talleon you look. If I hadn't been so mad at you I would have told you so." She shook her finger at him. "Anyway, we both look like him. We both look like Cyrenia. And we look like each other. We're twins after all. Green eyes, brown hair, and a nose like a chestnut." She ended by pinching and pulling on her nose.

"But males take after their father and females take after their mother. I look different from other Centaurs I know. I must look like father."

"My father, I mean our father. It's hard getting used to saying our when for so long it was just my father."

"I am having the same problem when I think of our mother. She never spoke of you directly but, I know that she never forgot you."

"How can you say that? Ladena had no idea I existed. You had no idea I existed. She walked away and never thought of me again. Our father told me all about you and her. He never forgot or let me forget." A harshness coated her words.

"I know she never forgot you because...come with me." He stood and led her out of the grove of trees to a clear patch of land open to the sky. Cyron pointed up at the brightest star in the sky. "What do you call that star?"

"That's the evening star; it's named 'Andra'." Every traveler, every sailor, every child knows that star. After the sun and the moon, it's the next thing you learn."

"When I was a very young colt," he said sitting on his hindquarters and staring up. "My mother, our mother, told me that our secret name for that star would be Talia. I knew it to be Andra and I thought it was strange, but I figured it was just a game she was playing. It was our secret name. What youngster doesn't like secrets? So, I played along. When she left on assignments she would say, "I'll be back before Talia rises." Or she'd get mad and say, "Not as long as Talia is in the sky." His voice became very soft. "I don't think she forgot you at all. As a matter of fact, I don't think she wanted me to forget you either, even if I didn't understand. Sometimes late at night I would find her staring at that star. Her eyes would be full of sadness. I would ask her what was wrong. She'd always say, "Talia is just so beautiful." The twins' eyes met. "I think she was right."

Teary eyed, Talia stared at the star. "She didn't forget me. She kept me with her, Cyron."

"Quiet," he whispered looking into the darkness.

"What is it?"

Peering through the black of the forest, he raised his hands to silence her. "Stay here." Cyron crept forward shielding himself behind a large tree. Scores of shadowed figures slithered by, moving toward the village. Cyron made his way back to Talia. "It's the Wolfmen, a lot of them. It may be the whole pack. They must be planning on attacking the village. I've got to warn them."

"You'll never get past them. There's too many of them."

"I've got to try. If I don't they could wipe out everyone."

Talia smiled. "It's a good thing you have a sister that's a Sorceress. You want a warning. I'll show you how to give a warning." They moved downwind and trailed the Wolfmen to the edge of the tree line overlooking the village.

"What are you going to do?" asked Cyron.

"Wait until they step out into the clearing. You'll see it's all in the hands. Just move back. I don't want to hurt you." Cyron took several steps backward. "Further," she waved him on. Reluctantly, he continued to move away until she nodded her approval.

As the Wolfmen emerged from the cover of the trees, Talia chanted her spell and gathered some of the energy around her. Whipping her arms about, she unleashed a barrage of loud, bright fireworks that raced into the sky turning the dark night into noontime brightness. The whole clearing was awash with bright light. The sudden noise and blinding light shocked the Wolfmen, halting their advance. The Centaurs, alerted by the noise and light, immediately spotted the approaching Wolfmen and sounded the alarm. Seconds later, the sky was filled with dozens of arrows driving the Wolfmen back. Squads of shielded and armored warriors rushed out of the village to do battle. Swords and spears clashed with claws and teeth. The night was filled with the cries of war.

Talia released another round of light explosions that helped the Centaurs root out the hiding and retreating Wolves. One of the Wolfmen spotted her. He charged her, baring long fangs and razor-sharp claws. As he leapt to strike her down, Cyron pulled his blade and launched himself at the charging creature. They met in midair. Cyron planted the point of his dagger deep into the Wolfman's chest. They both fell in a heap at Talia's feet.

"Cyron," she cried as she rushed to him. "Are you all right? Please, be all right. I just found you. I can't lose you already. Cyron, Cyron..."

Cyron pushed the dead Wolfman off him and asked in a jovial voice, "Are you always so emotional?" He smiled as she pushed him back and threw her arms around his neck. A shock, a charge passed between them. It caused them to jerk apart and stare at each other. The sounds of the battle drew their attention away. Cyron jumped to his feet picked up a nearby fallen spear and raced into the fighting. Talia kept the sky alight by hurling glowing balls that shot into the air hovered and burst in several directions, giving off bright shimmering light.

The surviving Wolves, overwhelmed and routed, escaped back into the forest disappearing into the shadows. Many laid dead on the battlefield. Those who were not dead were helped to get there. There was no doubt the night belonged to the Centaurs. The Wolves had suffered a crushing defeat. The village was alive with the celebration of victory. Battle always stirred the heart of a Centaur. Everyone, young and old, male and female, were out cheering and dancing with glee.

When Talia and Cyron returned to the village, they were met with praise and honors. Talia was singled out with words of encourage-ment and thanks. She had tried to get Hanar to accompany them. Despite Cyron's' assurance, he still feared he would be turned into a slave or a pet. "No," he said. "I'll feel safer out here."

Marreanus stood before the crowd giving a speech praising the city's defenses. Tyrel leaned over to Cyron. "See what I told you. Somehow he has managed to take credit for the victory." Cyron laughed.

Ladena leaned over and placed her hand on Talia's shoulder. "Your mother and your father would be so proud. I know I am."

CHAPTER 13

*P*halon sat at the table venting his frustration by stabbing and gouging the table with his knife. "Don't destroy the furniture," Cannullus said, entering the room and standing before the table. Phalon answered him by planting the knife deep into the wood. Cannullus dismissed the act of defiance. Phalon bared his canines. Cannullus dismissed this gesture as well.

Phalon narrowed his yellow eyes. He shifted tensely in the chair. His ears flickered, and his nose twitched as he sniffed the air. His body coiled tightly as if he was ready to strike. Phalon disliked the wizard, but understood he needed him. His disdain was evident by the contemptuous glares he gave Cannullus when he wasn't looking.

The wizard was a tall, thin man with a haughty air of authority. He had a habit of holding his head tilted up and looking down disapprovingly on everyone. Not using names and calling others by their trade was one of his ways of exercising his dominance. Emotionless pale brown eyes and a raspy voice made him appear displeased or indifferent to everything. There was an elegance in his features that was rendered artless and cold by his dismissive manner and the drabness of his mundane dress. Cannullus insisted on wearing only formless brown hooded robes made of drab coarse material. His show of modesty and humility was just another calculation in the facade he presented to those in power.

"My sources tell me," said Cannullus, "that your attack on the Centaur village did not go as planned. As a matter of fact, I am told it was a disappointing disaster."

Phalon growled and slammed his fist on the table. "They had a Witch to aid them. Everything was going as planned until she threw her magic into it. I lost many valuable members of my pack that night."

'A Witch?" Cannullus asked. Phalon nodded. "A young girl, green eyes, and auburn hair?"

Phalon nodded again. "That is her."

"So that is where she has got to."

"You know her?"

"Yes, Talia, the daughter of the late previous court Sorcerer."

"Too bad you didn't deal with them both when you had the chance. That would have taken care of both our problems." Cannullus gave him a warning stare, looking around as if he was afraid someone had heard Phalon's remarks.

"Magic or no magic, we need the Centaurs off that land. Kill them or drive them away. I don't care which one. That was our arrangement. We have given you substantial aid that has enabled you to grow and establish yourselves. I would hate to have to withdraw that support and leave you to fend for yourself."

"If you will fight with us, that will cancel out their advantage," Phalon added as a suggestion.

"No, that will not do. Firstly, we cannot be associated with this war or with you. To implicate the crown would cause havoc among the populace. I'm sorry to inform you, Phalon," he said staring intently at him. "but Wolfmen are not very popular with the common folk or any other folk, for that matter. Secondly, they not only have Talia, but the Shaman of their clan is very powerful in her own right. I would not want to cause them to unite their abilities. Thirdly, you have been paid handsomely to remove them. And lastly, the best course of action is to remove her from among them, not fight against her with them."

"You fear her," Phalon said with delight in his voice.

"Hardly," he replied with a tilt of his head. "She is a child. Perhaps, someday she may be quite powerful, but for now I have certain controls to keep her in line. Certain leverages at my disposal."

"Use them then. Get her to leave."

"No, that is for the future," he said and then mumbled to himself, "and for personal use." Cannullus focused a stern eye on Phalon. "It is not to be wasted to rescue you from your incompetence. The idea is to turn her to our way of thinking; to gain control of her, and by that, separate her from her new-found home. She must not be harmed." He insisted. "The crown has plans for her."

"I think, maybe," said Phalon with a sly glower. "you have plans for her."

Cannullus leaned on the table and stared at Phalon. He slapped the table with his palm. The knife dislodged, somersaulted through the air, and stuck itself into the chair between Phalon's legs. Phalon jerked back and grabbed the armrest in fright.

"Never presume to know my mind Phalon. Stick to what is your concern. Replenish your ranks and wait for further instructions. I will contact you in a few days." Cannullus pivoted and left the room.

Phalon stormed out of the castle, through back passages, with more anger than he had when he arrived. He exuded such a strong primal nature, it unnerved his horse. Despite the protest of the animal, he mounted and headed back to rejoin the pack, his mane of long black hair flapping in the wind as if it was trying to escape from his head. The coarse hair of his body bristled and stood on end making him look larger than he was. Yellow eyes violent with fury blazed like lanterns in the growing dark as he pushed the horse's speed to match his emotions.

"They think they can order me about and use me like an attack dog!" he yelled, a string of drool trailing from his lips. "Well, Cannullus, mighty court Wizard, the crown is not the only one with plans. I'll let you deal with the Witch while I..." he stood in the stirrups and pounded his chest.

"...I Phalon, leader of pack, will make some plans of my own. When this is over, we will see who has to fend for themselves. We'll see who rules whom."

Covering the distance with the speed of a raging fire, Phalon arrived at the abandoned silver mine that once was the home base for the pack. The horse, sweaty and frothing at the mouth, collapsed to the ground. The beast wheezed and died on the spot. Phalon ignored the animal and entered the cave. "Cybela, where are you?"

From the shadows, a small figure shrouded and hooded from head to toe, emerged. "There is such urgency in your voice, Phalon. What troubles the leader of the pack so?"

Phalon moved in close, hugging her to him. Removing the hood from her head, he whispered, "The time is coming soon, my Cybela. We need to make plans."

Cybela looked coyly into his eyes, a shadow of worry on her face. "This is a dangerous game you play, Phalon. Do not lose the moon in an attempt to capture the stars. The pack has grown and much has improved over the years. Is it wise to risk our continued survival in some wild dreams of revenge and conquest?"

"Since the great battle twenty years ago when we were defeated by the Centaurs and nearly wiped out, I have planned for their destruction." He narrowed his eyes and bared his canines. "I lost everything. All my family died that day." He pounded his clenched fist against his chest.

'I will have my revenge. So what if we use the Humans to get it? They have planned to use us to get rid of the Centaur. We have stood last in line for the last time. It is time for us to be first."

'What are you planning, Phalon?"

Phalon turned away and gave her a repentant sideways glance. "I need your help. We need an advantage in our struggle."

'You know I have nothing to offer you that would be of any use in your struggles, don't you? I have no powers of any use in battle. My contribution is piecing you back together after you have been sliced to shreds by a Centaur's sword." She raised her chin and swept her hand through her mane of thick black hair. "I am a creature of shapes and forms. My gift is a subtle one, and you, Phalon, are not a subtle creature."

The hairs on the back of his neck rose. "It is not as you suppose, Cybela." He cupped his hands behind his back and began pacing the dirt floor. "What if I could provide you with a source of power, a new power? Power that could aid us? Is there something you could do with that?"

Cybela raised a doubtful brow. "There is a young female, a Human female, a Sorceress, who has a powerful gift."

"Interesting," she purred her curiosity stirred. "...tell me more."

Phalon relayed all he knew of Talia, Cannullus, and Thangor, embellishing some parts and leaving out others. He chose his words carefully and kept his tone mild.

Cybela stroked her hairy chin and replied. "With the Centaurs' Shaman, Ladena, by her side it would be impossible to wrench this woman child from them. Do not underestimate Ladena. I have tangled with that old Shaman before. She is formidable. The girl could find no better mentor. And as you say the men of Mandoria want her return as well, so that will be another obstacle to overcome. This is not an easy task you ask me to surmount."

"Though the risk is great, so are the rewards. We can defeat the Centaurs and the Humans in one effort. In no time, we can again be the masters in this entire land." He moved in and embraced her. "You would be a queen." He bowed and looked up at her with a smile.

The She Wolf rubbed her hairy chin. Her eyes danced about weighing the possibilities. "If and I only say if you can find a way to separate her from the others, perhaps there are things that can be done. I have never done this myself. I have only heard of it. But, there are ways to take control of another. There is great uncertainty in it. I cannot be totally certain of what changes will come about. These things are difficult to control. Nor do I know if I can reverse their affects. Once this is attempted, if it is successful, it may be permanent. I may be a very different creature." She faced him her hands planted on her hips. "How would you like me as a Human woman? Would I still light the fire in that primitive heart of yours?"

"I would cherish you just as much, if not more." He pulled her to him. They shared a laugh and a passionate kiss.

Cybela retreated to her table. "I will make preparations. Keep me informed of any changes. When the time is right, I will be ready to act."

"In the meantime, I will go along with the plans of the castle." Phalon growled a smile. "I will love to see the smug face of that arrogant Cannullus when he has to bow at our feet."

CHAPTER 14

*W*hat excuses did that ignorant dog give for his bungling?" Thangor asked Cannullus as he entered his chambers.

"Talia was his excuse." Thangor's head sprang around in surprise. "It seems that our sweet little Talia has found herself a new home with the Centaurs."

"Talia, with the Centaurs?" Thangor asked, looking away from his image in the mirror.

"Yes, it appears that the rumors of her unusual birth may carry some truth. She is safe in the bosom of her people. It appears they have not only accepted her but embraced her as one of their own. The long-lost daughter returns home."

"I never should have let her out of here." Thangor gnashed his teeth. "We have to find a way to retrieve her."

"What do you suggest? Unfortunately, there is nothing here to tempt her back."

Thangor stopped and gave him a side way glance, not sure if he was being insulted or informed. "Everyone has a weakness," he said, retrieving his mirror. "Now that her father is dead something else has taken that place. Find out what it is, and we'll use it to bring our wayward Sorceress home. Start with that blacksmith. What's his name?"

'Barnabus," Cannullus said as if the name bored him.

'Yes, him. He was a friend with her father for many years. I'm sure he knows more than just how to shoe horses."

Cannullus bowed and left the room. *"I will find her weakness," he thought. "When I have control of her I will be able to eliminate yet another weakness. My vain Prince Thangor."*

$\mathcal{C}$annullus paced back and forth in front of Barnabus. The big man was bound to the wall of the dungeon, iron shackles clamped to his ankles and wrists. Dark bruises dotted his skin, and shredded and torn bloodstained clothes exposed deep cuts and lacerations all over his body. One of his eyes was swollen shut and a large gash over his brow dripped blood into the other. Barnabus' lips were swollen and split, leaking out a mixture of blood, saliva and an occasional tooth. He groaned as he slipped in and out of consciousness.

"Blacksmith," Cannullus said grabbing his hair and wrenching up his drooping head forcing Barnabus to look at him. "I do not enjoy this sort of thing. As a matter of fact, I find it rather barbaric. But your lack of cooperation gives me no other alternative. Simply tell me what I wish to know, and this will be over. You can return to wielding your hammer and I can proceed with more productive affairs."

"Bastard," Barnabus groaned.

"Bastard," Cannullus repeated. He paused, tilted his head as if listening for something. "I suppose you are right. After all, my mother was an ugly toothless old hag who haunted the docks. My father, probably was any one of hundreds of filthy drunken sailors who purchased her...shall we say, her services. So, I suppose I am a bastard." His voice dropped, and his expression hardened.

"As a bastard, I am called upon to do things that ones with a more noble lineage will not do. As you can imagine, this does not please me, but one does what one must." He lowered his eyes and sighed. "I plan to remedy this miscarriage of fate soon. But, that is for the future. We have something else to deal with first." A twisted smirk crested his face. He narrowed his stoic eyes and stared at Barnabus.

"My dear blacksmith, if you do not tell me what I request of you, I will be called to forcefully pull the information from your mind. It is an unpleasant process and it will leave you dead or something worse." He hesitated, looking at Barnabus with indifference, but Barnabus did not respond.

"Very well," he sighed and pulled a vial from his pocket. Grabbing the blacksmith's nose, Cannullus shut off his breathing, forcing him to open his mouth. Cannullus poured the concoction into his mouth. Barnabus tried to spit it out, but Cannullus slammed his fist into his chin causing him to close his mouth and swallow. Barnabus' one good eye grew wide with terror as if he had just been stabbed by a hot poker. He howled and began gasping violently. The chains rattled and clattered as he railed against his restraints. His body twisted and jerked banging into the wall.

Cannullus closed his eyes and smiled. Moments later the big man went limp. Cannullus raised Barnabus' eyelid and checked his condition. "Now Blacksmith, let's have a talk about our wayward little Talia. Tell me all you know about her."

In an emotionless, mindless monotone Barnabus relayed to the Wizard everything he knew about Talia's origins and her family. Cannullus delighted in the results. The blacksmith slumped on his chains, all his energy and knowledge expended.

Though he didn't have the magical talents of Talleon or Talia, Cannullus took great pride in his mastery of chemicals and herbs. His alchemy had served him well over the years, and he relished every chance he got to practice his art. Satisfied, he strutted out of the dungeon leaving the limp body of the dying man hanging like a dirty rag on a hook.

Equipped with the information needed, Cannullus made his way to his laboratory. With practiced fingers, he selected containers and began to carefully portion out various powders.

"Now my dear Prince, I think that it is time I add my plans to this equation." His voice was coated with contempt. "Once the little wench has been subdued and returned to the castle, I cannot allow you to control her. I have plans for our Talia. With you out of the way, it will be no problem to coerce her into total submission to me and me alone. Who knows? I may even marry and impregnate her. After all the new king must have a royal heir." His laughter bubbled up like the boiling liquid in one of his laboratory flask.

"Phalon will undoubtedly be a problem. What am I going to do with that beast? I can't kill them all, even though nothing would please me more. I will have to reach some accommodation with him and his pack I suppose. I guess even the best plans have their flaws."

"So, there is a mother and a brother," Thangor tried on another robe and admired himself in the mirror. "...either one will do for our purposes. What did you learn about them?"

"It appears the mother is just your ordinary female Centaur, but the boy, being her twin and partially human, has certain un-Centaur-like qualities. Barnabus actually did not see him, but he was told that the boy has human ears, no horns, and a hairless body. From the waist up, he looks very Human. Quite the mix."

"H-m-m," moaned Thangor. "Do you think this would be appropriate for mother's birthday party?" He asked, primping before the mirror surrounded by a growing pile of discarded apparel.

"Most appropriate, I'm sure," Cannullus answered quickly not even looking, refusing to play wardrobe mistress.

"Why am I asking you for fashion advice?" Thangor asked laughing. "Look at that thing you wear. What is it, a flour sack?"

Cannullus accepted the insult with an expressionless stare of no concern. "My convictions demand modesty." Thangor laughed. Cannullus ignored him and continued.

"I will need to go to the Wolves stronghold," he said. "Phalon and I will devise a plan to acquire one or both of them."

"Go, but I want to be there when that little fish bites. I will join you at the stronghold in seven days. Make sure Phalon is expecting me. Talia and I have much unfinished business to resolve. I want to be there when she begs for the return of her animal relations. I want to see her finally realize that her fate is in my hands. The very thought that I would want her anyway is absurd, but there is..."

"The magic," Cannullus finished his thought.

"Yes Wizard. You of all people would understand about the magic. Your skills," he said the word reluctantly. "with potions and elixirs have been useful. I suppose we have to reward you for the years of service you have given as the second to that self-righteous Talleon." He raised his brows and gave Cannullus a knowing smile.

"How convenient of him to die and make room for you." His smile widened. A slight tilt of his head followed. "But, with Talia there is real power, real magic. As my bride, her talents will be at my total disposal. None would dare oppose any move I make. If only her father had been more amiable. Those worrisome Centaurs would have been wiped from the land by now and we wouldn't have to deal with those filthy Wolves."

He added: "She is untested. Her possible abilities, I grant you may have potential, but she does not have the will."

"It does not matter if she has the will. I do. Besides she seems to have enough will to defeat your Wolfmen."

"They are not *my* Wolfmen."

"I seem to recall you were the one who came to me with the idea of using them to our ends. I agreed yes, but they have been, and will always remain your Wolfmen, your problem."

Cannullus ignored the assertions and continued to talk of Talia. "To yield such a gift and not realize its potential is sacrilege."

"Cannullus, you are so transparent. Your envy and jealousy are so evident. Just because her powers eclipse yours many times over is no reason to vilify her. It is just the luck of the wheel. You are a skilled alchemist and she is a gifted Sorceress."

Thangor sought to offer him a consolation. "You need not worry about Talia. She will be my own personal concern." He looked over his shoulder and added as an afterthought, "Your position will be secure. You will remain the official court Alchemist. Oh sorry, I meant court

'Wizard' with all that it entails. She will be exclusively my concern, not yours..."

Thangor mumbled as he turned away. "even though you are yet to produce any chemical miracles."

Cannullus absorbed the remark pretending he did not hear it. "Of course, your Highness. Thank You. I was just anticipating your wants." he said with a bow.

"Even though as you say the Wolves are my problem, I would not want to make a decision without your input. Have you given any thought to the problem of Phalon? Once the Centaurs have been removed, we will still have the Wolves to contend with. I am very suspicious of Phalon. I believe that he has larger aspirations in mind."

"Larger aspirations for what?" Thangor laughed. "You give them too much respect. The Wolves are savages. They're animals. All they know is claw, bite, and kill. As long as we give them some far off land to run wild in like the uncivilized beasts they are, what more could they ask for? Phalon is useful at best, and a temporary irritation at worst." He waved off the idea and donned another robe. "After all, why would you ask me about your problem? As I said earlier, you brought them in, you find a way to dispose of them."

Cannullus raised his brows concealing his anger behind an expressionless facade and bowed out of the room. "As you wish, Your Highness." As a closing thought, he added, "But even a dog wants more than just a bone, sometimes, Your Highness." Thangor wrapped himself in silk and linen and ignored him.

CHAPTER 15

*C*yron bounded nosily into the yard, still full of the energy from the festivities of the night before.

"Quiet, Cyron. Talia is still sleeping. It took a lot of energy to produce her magic last night. She needs to regain her strength. Go home and let her rest." Ladena scolded from her perch beside the front door.

"She's not sleeping," said Cyron. "she's getting dressed."

"What makes you think...?" Before she could finish her thought, Talia stepped out of the door.

"I told you," he said, looking at a questioning Ladena. "I've come to take you somewhere special."

Talia smiled and nodded. "I know. I've been waiting." Ladena watched the exchange bewildered.

"We'll be back later," Cyron said, trotting east toward the hills. Passing the cemetery, they both looked to Cyrenia's grave, sharing a silent moment of understanding. When they came to the beginning of the foothills, Cyron left the path and veered behind a stand of trees. "It takes a little effort to get to, but it's worth the trouble." He stepped over a waist-high wall of rocks, then under an outcropping in the hill. Passing, finally, through a short tunnel that opened out onto a garden.

A trickling waterfall pooled into a small clear pond. Lush grasses laid out like a living blanket. Vibrant colored flowers sprouted in random bunches. Vines scaled the hills and purple mosses laid a winding trim around the space. "Cyron, this is lovely!" Talia danced in circles, taking in the idyllic scene.

'I knew you would like it. This is my special place, my quiet place. I used to come here a lot when I was younger. After a day of getting trampled, gored, and made fun of this was where I would come to find some peace. I tried to run away once. That's how I found this place, by accident,'

Cyron sighed. "It wasn't so easy growing up with these ears..." He flicked them with his hands. "and no horns." His face had lost all expression.

"How about growing up with these ears..." Talia pulled her hair back, exposing her cloven ears. "...and these horns?" She revealed her buds.

"Huh, so that's where they went to. I sure could have used those growing up. They would have saved me from getting into a lot of fights."

"And I could have used yours. Human ears would have saved me a lot of tears. The other children were so cruel. They used to tease me unmercifully. I felt like a..."

"An outsider. A freak." he said. She nodded.

"Poor father and Barnabus had to dry buckets of tears."

"Who's Barnabus?"

"Uncle Barnabus."

"You mean I have an Uncle too?"

"No. Not really. Well...sort of. He's father's best friend. He's a blacksmith. I call him 'Uncle' because he was always there, and he was so good to me."

"I guess neither of us had it easy growing up. It's not easy with your feet in two worlds. At least you knew what was going on. Mother never told me anything. She would just say I was different for a reason and one day that reason would be made clear to me. That's not a whole lot of comfort when you have to fight your way through every day."

"Father told me, but said I had to keep it a secret because people wouldn't understand. I took great care to try and hide these ears, but sometimes I couldn't and..." She looked away from him.

He finished the thought for her. "The rejection hurts. The feeling that you aren't wanted. That you don't belong. Even though I managed to make it." Cyron paused and swallowed. "I've never told anyone this, but I have never really felt like I belonged. If I didn't have mother and Ladena, I don't think I would have stayed."

"I know the feeling. Father and Barnabus were my shields. At least with them around I wasn't too lonely. It was hard for me to make friends. Magic saved me. I spent most of my time in father's laboratory, or with my head in a book." Each child, in his or her own way understood the pain of the other. No more words were necessary. They sat and watched the waterfall.

"Talia, tell me about my father. Cyrenia always said my father died in the war. I knew his name was Talleon. She wouldn't talk about him anymore than that. Nobody else knew who he was, not even Ladena. I was left to make him up."

Cyron looked off into the distance, his dream playing in front of him. "I always thought he was a Centaur like me, and that he was as a great warrior." He placed his fist against his waist and puffed out his chest. "A wanderer who happened on to the battlefield. Someone who came to the aid of his distant brethren and died in the glory of war." His chest deflated. "That didn't explain the ears and the horns, but it helped."

Talia smiled and eagerly began a lengthy recital of Talleon, her father being one of her favorite subjects. She reveled in relaying all she could think about him.

"He was the wisest, kindest person I've ever known. And, he was the most talented Sorcerer in the land," she went on and on, telling Cyron about Mandoria, the castle, Barnabus, Thangor and Cannullus. Cyron sat in wonderment, not knowing anything, but the village and the forest around it.

"I always dreamed about seeing other places."

"Me too. The stories father told me about his travels made me curious to see them all."

"You've seen a lot more than me."

"Not really. Only Mandoria and here. Father always promised when I got older he would..." Her words trailed off.

"Talia," Cyron's voice became soft and low. "How did Father die?"

The question caused her back to stiffen and the air to catch in her throat. Talia's cheeks flushed, and her breath became rapid. Her eyes darted about looking for an escape. The pounding of her heart was so loud she felt it in her ears. "He...he...he..." She stuttered.

"That's all right. I didn't mean to upset you. I can see that the wound is still too fresh. We can talk about that another time."

Talia hung her head more in shame than sorrow. *I can't tell him,* she thought. *He'll know I'm to blame. He'll hate me. I just can't. No one but Cannullus can know my secret. No one.* The fear of knowing one day she would have to reveal the truth made her heart ache. The thought of losing her newfound family scared her. She sunk into silence.

"What did you say?" Cyron asked.

"I didn't say anything."

"I thought I heard you say something about secrets." He shrugged his shoulders.

Talia tensed. *What if he knows I'm hiding something? What can I do?* Talia rubbed her forehead. *I've got to be careful. He can't find out.* Talia leaned back and eased her breathing.

Cyron gave her a hesitant glance and asked. "Is Hanar your...you know? If he is, it's alright," Cyron was holding up his hands as if he were surrendering. "I mean you being my sister and all. I just wanted to know."

Talia gave him a startled look and smiled. "What is this? Protecting your sister from a broken heart?" She managed a giggle. "No, he's just a friend, someone I've grown to care about and cherish. I'm not ready to give you a brother yet."

"Are you hungry?" asked Cyron, going to a string of vines. "This place comes with its own marketplace. There are berries over here and apples over there..." He pointed to a small tree bearing yellow fruit. "And I'm sure there are more delights I haven't even found." They ate and washed up in the pond.

"Cyron, did you feel something last night? That jolt when we touched?" asked Talia.

He gave her a sideways glance. "Yes. I felt something. What was it?" he asked through a mouth full of apple.

"I don't know. But, today I knew when you were on the way to Ladena's as sure as if you told me you were coming."

Cyron spit out a seed. "I was sure you were up and about. Even now, when we were just sitting quietly, I thought I could faintly hear you talking even when you weren't. What does it mean?"

"I've got an idea, but I need to talk it over with Ladena. I think it's time we got back. I want to check on Hanar." As they returned to the village, Talia thoughts turned again to worry. *Can he read my thoughts? Can I read his?* She closed her eyes and tried. *I have to be careful. I have to keep my secrets.*

CHAPTER 16

*I*n the ramshackle ruins of the abandoned mining town, Cannullus strategized with Phalon. "You have seen the boy?"

"Yes, out on patrol with the others. He is as you say, different. He stands out from the rest."

"And the mother?"

"It is difficult to say. The others look the same. There is no way to tell which she is, especially when they are shielded in armor."

"Then we will concentrate on the boy. I will mix you a sleeping potion that will render him unconscious. Something you can dip your claws in so that a scratch will do the job." Cannullus smiled, potions were his specialty and he enjoyed concocting deadly brews.

"It will be your task to subdue him and bring him back here. Alive and unharmed," he added with a threatening stare.

"Then what?" grunted Phalon.

"You need not worry about that. We have a plan in hand. Just get him here and have your pack guard him. Do not harm him. Do you understand? At least not until we have the girl cooperating."

"Don't talk down to us, Cannullus. We are not your pet hounds to be ordered about and used like beasts of burden. You make plans and leave us out. You make decisions and don't consider us. We are supposed to be allies, not servants." Phalon beat his chest. "We take all the risks and do all the work. My pack mates and I are not subjects of your kingdom. We do not grovel before men as you do."

"Why Phalon, of course we are allies. I am sorry if my concentration on my duties has left you with the impression that we do not value our association. You are an asset and will be duly compensated at the appropriate time." He gave his most practiced smile. Cannullus read the mistrust in Phalon's eyes and realized that despite Thangor's dismissiveness, the Wolves and their leader would not be content with just some land to run free. The prince and Phalon would both have to be handled carefully, but maybe he could find a way to make them cancel each other out. The thought gave Cannullus a pleasant thrill. With an oily smile, he offered the dog a bone.

"To show how much we appreciate you and your people, I've convinced Prince Thangor to come meet with you personally. Not at the castle, of course. We still have to maintain a certain amount of discretion. But, he will be arriving here in four days. Could you arrange some suitable accommodations for him?" He looked around with a doubting frown.

"The crown is coming here? At last you begin to show us some respect. This is good." Phalon thought an advantage for him must lie in this somehow, and he had every intention of using it. The idea of dealing with the crown instead of Cannullus was pleasing. "Our needs are simple, but I will see what can be done." Cannullus consumed with the squalor of his surroundings, did not notice the calculating grin of Phalon.

"When the prince comes we can talk of this compensation you speak of..."

"Yes, yes," interrupted Cannullus waving away the complaint. "The prince and I are aware of your needs. We will fulfill our part of the bargain, but first we must acquire the girl, and of course eliminate the Centaurs. Then and only then," he held up a finger. "will you get the things that you need." Cannullus ran a finger across the dusty table. "I can see that your needs are great. Why don't you start with cleaning this place up?"

Phalon banged his clenched fist on the table. "We need weapons for war and tools for building, not brooms and mops. We are warriors, not chamber maids. My pack has suffered at the hands of the Centaurs and the Humans alike. Forced to forage like wild beasts. We are not wild beasts. We once knew greatness. We will know it again. Our numbers grow and soon we will be what we were. My kind was here before the Humans and the Centaurs. We will have our lands back. When you came to us with this bargain, you made promises." Phalon's mouth twisted with the words. "We will not be denied again."

Phalon paced around the room, a growl growing in his chest. "After the great war," he continued, "our numbers were few. We had to hide and avoid the other races. You..." he turned to Cannullus and snarled. "...you hunted us like rabbits, but we are strong and many now. We are the ones doing the hunting." A grin lifted the corners of his mouth, displaying sharp wet fangs.

Cannullus stretched to his full height. "Don't think you can threaten me, Phalon. If you like, I can return to the castle and leave you and yours to deal with the Centaurs without our assistance. With the addition of their newest member, I am sure they will make quick work of you."

Phalon's face broke into a full smile. "I know you will not do this. I know you want the girl, and we can get her for you." Phalon narrowed his eyes until they were thin slits. "You are a clever one, Cannullus. The castle has plans, but do they know that you have plans also? I do not think that your plans and the castle's plans are the same. The girl, I have seen your eyes when you speak of her. You have plans for her." Cannullus stiffened. "I do not care what your plans are, Wizard. It only matters to me what is in this for us. Do your deeds but know that we will have our reward one way or the other."

"I have underestimated you, Phalon." Cannullus stroked his chin and gave the Wolfman a cautious stare. "I see that your understanding of the situation is better than I thought. All right, you will have your weapons on the condition that you carry out our plans. As a good faith gesture, I will arrange the delivery of a small shipment with the prince."

Phalon licked his lips and nodded his agreement.

CHAPTER 17

*L*adena and Talia spent a great deal of time together talking and practicing magic. There were new spells, new incantations, new potions, and valuable advice to be had. Talia asked questions, and Ladena provided answers. Talia found new ways of understanding things. Her grandmother, much to her delight, turned out to be an endless source of knowledge. The old Centaur was eager to share her experience and was gentle in her instruction. She had a familiarity with things that even Talia's father had only a passing comprehension of.

"There is magic, but there is also common sense," Ladena said. "If you think before you act and think before you speak, it is surprising just how much of that is mistaken for wisdom or magic."

Ladena in turn was impressed with the young woman's knowledge and skill. Her natural grasp of things, the easy way she handled new magic, and the enthusiasm she had for the art all together.

"Your father is to be commended. He has indeed instructed you very well. It's rare that I have encountered one so young and yet as talented and well versed as yourself." Ladena chuckled. "I also enjoy the dramatic waving of your hands when you display your abilities."

"Father called it hand dancing." She blushed and giggled with the memory. "It is something I've been doing ever since I was a young girl. I was always so nervous when doing magic. I didn't know what to do with my hands, so it just kind of happened."

"Yes, that is a good name for it. And you dance very well." Ladena winked at her. "We all find our own particular way of doing things." She stood rigidly and stared into Talia's eyes. "We all have our requirements to perform; our own path to the magic." She sighed. "When I act, the world becomes silent to me."

"Silent?" Ladena nodded. "You don't hear anything?" Talia asked.

"I only hear the music of my magic. And it is a lovely song. It's as if the universe is a lyre and I am strumming my song. All else is silent to me. This is the way of my magic."

"I just get very tired. Sometimes I can sleep for days. Father used to be very hungry after doing magic. Sometimes he would eat enough for a family of four." She giggled at the memory.

"That is the toll of the magic. Everyone has a unique reaction. Most are just like you, they get very weary from the spent energy, but to each his own."

"I don't mind. I grew up in Father's workshop. Ever since I can remember, magic has been a big part of my life. I can't imagine my life without it. We spent long hours and many wonderful days experimenting and practicing magic."

Talia rose up on her toes as if the memories were lifting her off the ground. "I read volumes of books. Anything I could get my hands on. If I found something I did not understand, father would take the time to explain it until I understood. He was a very kind and patient teacher and I was an eager student. We studied everything; there were no subjects off limits to me. So, you see magic has always been with me. I could not exist without it."

"Life is magic." Ladena replied. "There is the magic of life itself and then there is the magical life. We all have life, so we all have magic. Everything has a little magic, a little bit of the divine in it. Some things and some creatures are magical; such as crystals, Dragons, Fairies, and even some places are magical. These things are born of magic; born of wonder and mystery." She waved her hands and a rainbow of light arched in the room. "Magic lives. Magic is personal. Your father had..."

"The magic of making." Talia jumped in, enthusiastically. "He was a creator. He could make the most unusual and fascinating things. Once when I was a little girl, he joined a mouse and a bird. It had leathery wings and flew. It was wonderful. He once did a trout and a dog. It tried to bark underwater and nearly drowned. That one didn't work out so well."

Talia was that excited little girl again. She glowed with the happiness of her memories. "He used to make me the most beautiful flowers to cheer me up whenever I was sad. Some of them glowed in the dark and chimed when you blew on them. He could make the most beautiful things, Ladena. I wish you could have seen them."

"Indeed, child," Ladena smiled at her exuberance, enjoying the glimpse of the little girl she had never known.

Her expression darkened as if a cloud had come to block out the sun. "Sometimes he made horrible frightening things with fangs and claws and bloody red eyes, things out of nightmares." She bristled at the thought. "Sometimes his creations scared me out of the laboratory."

"I have the gift of growth and healing, of renewal. It is natural for me to see the promise of life where others only see decay and death. It is no accident that you see so much life and death around me. It is who I am. I deal in life, but as with all things there is death on the other side. There can be no life without it. Take this to heart child, there must be loss to have gain. Not all that we see as dark is evil, and not all that we see as light is good. There must be a balance. Too much of anything, even a good thing can be bad. Equal parts preserve the balance."

She paused and gave Talia a peculiar stare as if she had just awakened and had to remember who she was. "How much power can you channel? Have you tested the limits?"

Talia tensed. Her eyes grew wide and she became visibly anxious.

"I see that you have," nodded Ladena. "Do not fear the power child.

You must learn to understand it and its limits. It is a gift. It is only when we misuse our gifts that we should worry. Now, tell me."

Talia began pacing. Her skin began to heat. A bead of sweat ran down her back and her throat tightened up. "Months ago," her voice faltered. She sat and fumbled with her hands. Talia swallowed and began again. "A few months ago, father wanted to see how much power I could channel. He had me meditate on it all the morning. That afternoon we went down to the quarries where they shape the great blocks of stones to build and repair the outer walls of the castle. I was to concentrate on a great mountain of a stone. The block was larger than this house. I was supposed to direct all the power I could gather on it. We assumed I would chip off a part of it. I..."

Her voice grew high and thin. "I gathered all the energy around me. It was frightening because I had never felt so much power at one time. I concentrated and released it at the stone. It shattered to dust. The whole thing." Her eyes grew wide as if it was happening before her. "When the dust cleared, I turned to Father. I was frightened and excited all at once. I thought Father would be pleased. His expression was one of shock and worry. I thought I had done something wrong. But, it wasn't me. It was who else he saw. Thangor and Cannullus had been watching us from a hill top. I didn't understand for a while why he was so upset until he began talking to me about being controlled by others."

"I understand why your Prince wants to..."

"He's not my Prince." She snapped, stomping her feet and beginning to pace again.

Ladena smiled. "I see why they wish to have influence over you. You are very powerful my child, and you will only become more so as you mature. To control such forces could be a mighty weapon for anyone."

"I will not be anyone's weapon." She yelled at her feet quickening her pace. "I am not a tool to be wielded like a sword or to be pushed around like a broom. I will not be used by anyone. This is my life, and I will choose how to live it."

"I am happy to hear that, but you must understand your gift, not run from it. Your power of channeling flows not only from the part of you that is human, but also from the part of you that is a Centaur. You have a heritage of magic in you. You have your father's line and you have my line. My mother and her mother before her, as far back as can be remembered; we were Shamans. It skipped your mother." Ladena smiled. "We feared the line was broken. I thought I would be the last. Your mother always was more like her father than me. But, happily the line has reappeared in you."

Ladena hesitated to form a question. "Have you ever thought of directing energy to another purpose? I would bet you couldn't only use your gift to destroy, but to build." Talia gave her a puzzled look.

"The balance," she offered. "...embrace that duality. I am sure you have the ability. You carry two spirits. Discover the other one. Be them both and you will be even more powerful. No one will be able to control you," she hesitated as her gaze drifted to the window.

"Cyron has gifts as well. I'm sure of it. I never considered the possibility until now. He has never discovered them. They have never openly manifested themselves" She tilted her head. "Perhaps that explains his uncanny ability with a bow and arrow. I have seen him shoot an arrow and that arrow bend in midair to find its target. We all considered it was his keen eyesight. He is only half Centaur and yet he can best anyone he encounters." Ladena looked off into the distance, hunched her shoulders, and continued.

"Anyway, he is not as focused as you, so he will never reach your level. But do not under estimate him. One day his abilities will make themselves known."

Talia kept pacing. "There is something else, is there not?" Ladena asked. Talia stopped and covered her face with a fist full of hair. The thought of her secret being exposed made her head hurt and her stomachache with guilt.

"Yes, something happened with your power. It has frightened you. Someone was hurt? Is that why you hold back and look so apprehensive when you use your magic?"

Talia stood frozen as if her legs had turned to stone. *She knows,* she thought. Her heart began to race. All she wanted to do was run and hide.

"Worry not child," the old shaman said. "I will not pressure you to reveal your secrets. I will wait until you want to tell Ladena."

"Oh Ladena, I did something awful." She laid her head on Ladena's shoulder. "I don't deserve to have magic. I...I."

"Now, now," she said stroking Talia's hair. "Your heart is pure. Whatever happened was not meant to do harm. Take solace in your intentions. Things will have their way. It may yet be revealed that you are not so much to blame as you think. Magic has a way of doing what it is supposed to do regardless of what you want it to do."

Ladena wiped her eyes and kissed her on the forehead. "A cup of tea will soothe your nerves. Then we can move on to happier things."

After tea and honey bread swabbed with butter, Talia had calmed and returned to herself. Sitting on a stool next to Ladena, she asked, "Grandmother, the other night during the battle, Cyron and I...well I thought he was hurt and I hugged him. Something passed between us. A spark, a shock of some kind. Then the next day...I don't know how to explain it, but I knew when he was near. It's almost like I was in his head. He has said the same thing of me. What could it mean?"

Ladena laughed. "Do you not already know? After all, you two shared a womb together. What makes you think that minds that have been so closely linked and touched by magic as well, can ever really be separated?"

"What are you saying? That we can read each other's minds?"

"Not exactly or should I say not yet. Just that you are connected. Being brought back together has revived that bond. Unspoken words and experiences will be shared between you, be experienced by you both. The stronger the emotions, the stronger the link. Over time, who knows? You may be able to read or even talk to each other without uttering a word."

Ladena closed her eyes and sighed. "I must rest now child; magic does not come to me as easily as it used to. Later this evening we will discuss more." She held up her hand to stop the forming questions.

"Later."

CHAPTER 18

*W*hile on patrol, Cyron stopped to check on Hanar. The Satyr had gotten a little more comfortable with him but was still cautious about him coming alone.

"I promised Talia I would stop in to make sure you were all right. She's busy with Ladena and couldn't get away today. Is everything all right?"

Hanar shook his head with an apprehensive shifting of his eyes. He tried to manage a smile, but his fear wouldn't let him. He stood balancing on his toes like a runner ready to breakout into a sprint.

"Come on, Hanar. When are you going to forgive me and let us be friends? I said I was sorry. I really meant it."

Hanar relaxed and collapsed to the ground. "I know. It's just that my father told me how he was almost made a slave by the Centaurs. He used to tell me stories before I went to sleep every night; stories about Fairies and Trolls and Giants and Centaurs. Some were so scary that I would stay up all night scared something would come and take me away."

"Did you ever think that maybe he made those stories up?"

"No. Well...maybe."

"After all, you were just a sapling. Maybe he was just trying to entertain you or scare you so you'd be more careful?"

"I suppose you could be right. But, I'm still not going into that village. Just to be on the safe side."

"Alright, as long as we can be friends."

Hanar smiled and shook his head. "Cyron, I did want to talk to you." He moved closer and lowered his voice. "You know the Wolves keep an eye on the village, don't you?" Cyron nodded. "Day and night, there are always some of them sneaking around. They spy on the village. I spy on them. I keep a close eye on them. I'm very good at becoming part of the forest. They never even know I'm around. I can be a tree, a bush, or a shadow." Hanar puffed up his chest, obviously proud of his stealth. Hanar leaned in even closer. His voice was just above a whisper.

"I overheard them talking. They plan on capturing someone. I believe it is Talia, because they're always growling about the "Witch" and what they'll do to her. There's a lot of anger about what she did the night of the attack. I'm afraid for her, Cyron. We have to protect her."

"Don't worry," Said Cyron. "I'll keep a close eye on her. They won't get anywhere near her. Once I report this to Marreanus, I'm sure we'll increase the patrols."

*C*yron reported what Hanar had told him and Marreanus agreed to increase the patrols.

"We shouldn't be sitting around waiting for another attack. I think it's time we took the fight to the Wolves. We're warriors, not guard dogs," Tyrel said.

"He might be right," added Cyron. "Maybe it's time to deal with them once and for all."

Marreanus looked at the two young bucks. He understood the call of action that beat in their young hearts. The passion for battle, the need to prove one's self. The heated blood of a warrior was not new to him. He had felt it himself at one time, when the only life he put in jeopardy was his own, but that was before he became the leader. Now he was responsible for many lives, and his blood no longer ran so hot. Despite his hesitation, he couldn't help but feel pride and even a little envy at the younger version of himself he saw in his son.

Marreanus also understood the reality of war. An all-out war with the Wolves could be devastating to the Centaur. With their dwindling numbers, a direct assault could pose a serious risk to their future. It could deplete their ranks to the point they couldn't protect the village. Real life held real consequences, not just the glorious adventures the young envisioned. Despite the Centaurs' skill at war, the Wolves were formable enemies. No, a measured approach was needed, not youthful enthusiasm. "We'll hold a council meeting and discuss it. We can't rush blindly into war without a strategy to win. For now, let's just expand the patrols and make sure everyone stays alert."

"We can't talk the Wolves away," Tyrel snapped.

"You'll learn my son, there is more to war than dreams of glory."

Tyrel puffed out his chest. "I've fought in battles before. I understand what war is. We can't just sit back and let the Wolves ambush us and pick us off one by one. We need to put an end to them and this conflict."

Marreanus' nostril flared. He narrowed his eyes and stomped his hoofs against the wooden floor. "I am leader of this clan. A colt will not chastise me. There is more to war than your need for glory, Tyrel. Go out on your patrol and leave leadership to those with wiser, cooler heads."

"Maybe Tyrel is right. Talia is in danger." Cyron bit his lip. "So is the village," he added. "She's one of us, now. We have a duty to look out for her." The words caught in his throat. "I have a duty. She's my sister!"

Marreanus locked a cold stare on the pair. Tyrel pranced in place as if he was about to bolt from the room. Cyron froze in place, his chest heaving like a bellow. "We do owe her a debt," Marreanus started. "But, I have to think about the fate of all, not just the misfortune of one. We cannot act without forethought."

"She's in danger! The Wolves are vicious! Her magic can't protect her from all of them! She needs our help!" Cyron insisted.

Tyrel, finding courage in Cyron's words, stepped forward to speak. Marreanus silenced the room by rearing up on his back legs and coming down with a deafening stomp.

"Enough!" he shouted. "I will not risk all for the sake of your Human. My decision is final." Rushing forward, he met the young stallions face-to-face, his nostrils flaring like a bird's wings.

"Unless you wish to challenge me for the leadership of the clan." Cyron and Tyrel shrank back in silence. "If you are so troubled go to your post and make sure the Wolves do not darken our door."

Overflowing with a mixture of anger and fear, Cyron bristled and stomped from the room. Tyrel followed, shooting accusatory stares at his father.

CHAPTER 19

*L*adena, I know what my abilities are. All I do is channel the energy around me. Direct it. I can't give life."

"Of course, you can't, silly child." Ladena said, as if the idea was ridiculous. "Only the Great Maker can give life, but what I'm sure you can do is direct the energy of life where it is needed, nourishing what is there and helping it to grow and heal. As females, we cradle life. That is something males cannot understand. Your father was an impressive Sorcerer, but he was male, a man. There are things that males cannot understand. We as females have the ability to conceive life within us. The males marvel at it and are even afraid of it, because they can never truly understand it. Life is energy and you channel energy. You must change the way you see that energy. It is meant not only for destruction, but also for construction. You can use it to revitalize and repair, if you direct it properly."

With frustration in her voice, Talia said, "I don't see how I can possibly do that. Father never even mentioned anything like that."

"Your father, good man that he was, did not have all the facts, as I do." She punctuated her statement with a stern look and a tap to her forehead.

"Look here," said Ladena, moving to a potted flower. "I am sorry my little friend." She spoke to the plant as she would a babe. "The child here needs your help." She took a knife and sliced a sliver from the thick stem. Sap oozed down the stem. Cupping the stem with the palm of her hand, she whispered a prayer. When she removed her hand, the cut had been healed. The stem looked smooth and untouched. Moving to another pot holding a young budding plant she turned to Talia. "Now you do it."

"But, I can't," Talia pleaded. Ladena held up her hand and gave her the look of a nanny displeased with her charge. Talia's actions said, "yes ma'am" without saying a word. Ladena sliced the stem, apologizing to it in turn.

"Now, wrap your hand gently around the wound. Hold it as you would a newborn chick. Don't draw the energy from around you the way you have been taught to do, but from within you, ever so slowly and softly."

Talia tentatively gripped the wounded stem. "I am sorry little flower. I will try to make it better." Ladena smiled and nodded her approval.

"Close your eyes and just feel the plant. Don't do anything yet, just concentrate."

Talia closed her eyes. After a few seconds, she began to frown and released the stem. "It's hurting. I felt the pain."

"Of course, it is. It has been wounded and is bleeding its life away. You must ignore the pain and give it the energy it needs to heal. Now try it again, and this time look past the pain to its wellness."

Talia once again cupped the stem, closed her eyes, and grimaced. The pain the plant felt softly rippled through her hand and up her arm. It was not severe, but it was intense. She said a silent prayer to the maker of all things and concentrated on repairing the flower. The flow of energy she felt was unlike anything she had ever felt. It was like sunshine warming the back of her hand. The pain eased and she relaxed. The energy continued to flow, warm and soothing. She began to smile.

"Stop! That's enough!" The shout shocked her out of her concentration. Talia released the plant and opened her eyes. She immediately stepped back in surprise. The plant had not only been healed, but had flowered and grown a foot.

'Very, very impressive," Ladena laughed slapping her hocks and taking a seat. "You child...you may one day become legend." She chuckled with pride. Talia looked at the plant, unable to speak.

After a cup of tea and some gentle teasing form Ladena, Talia relaxed and felt more like herself. "We will practice more tomorrow. I will take you with me when I visit the sick. You will get a chance to work on something other than a plant. Just don't make whoever you encounter into a giant as you did the plant. I don't think they would like that very much." She chuckled and Talia flushed with embarrassment.

"Now, one last thing for today." She stared at Talia directly in the eyes with an expression that relayed her seriousness. "The Fire," said Ladena, "...is that point where your magic becomes more than you. It overwhelms you, it consumes you," she shook her head, "...like a flood. The power no longer comes from you or through you, but because of you. It takes on a life of its own. It emanates from the essence of all things. It is like holding hands with the gods."

Ladena's eyes narrowed, and her voice became as sharp as a warning siren. "When you reach such a point, you are transformed. It takes you. The Fire and you are one. What remains after could be anything. You may still be you. Or you could be made anew. Or you could be dead, burned up in the flames of your own light. Consumed by the flame of your own life."

"Father spoke of such a thing many times. He warned me of being seduced by the power. He said that I must never surrender to it. He said it wasn't evil, but it could lead to evil. According to him, it cannot be controlled. That all who have reached for it have eventually been destroyed."

"Indeed, he was right. I only speak of it because I can see that your magic lives in the light of those flames. I have known those who have tried for it, but they did not have your potential. Their efforts were in vain, unlike you, someone whose power will grow with age and experience. Allowing your mind and heart to run rampant can cause you to fall into its grasp. Ultimate power is so tempting. The idea of making the world as you want it; considering yourself equal to the gods. You are gifted and have great ability. Guard yourself well. Be wary Talia. Power is seductive. It alters the way we think and feel. Be cautious that your emotions don't overwhelm you and lead you down a path to destruction. Temper your desire. Rein in your emotions. Do not be tempted by the possible. Many have not heeded the warning," she hesitated. "They met horrible ends."

"Ladena, what is The Fire really?"

"No one really knows. No one completely understands. But, it is ancient, as old as time itself. It is the basis of all things, and the beginning and the end of all life. Some say it is a direct connection to the gods. The blessing of their grace is bestowed upon you. Some think it is the energy of life itself erupting from the center of the universe. Some call it the soul of god."

Ladena fell back into a sitting position. "No one knows for sure. All we can be certain of is The Fire is the ultimate power in the universe. It is what magic is made of. Every time you use your abilities you are channeling a tiny part of it."

CHAPTER 20

I hope I never become as old and nervous as Marreanus. If I didn't know better, I would think he was afraid. When I'm the leader of the clan, I'll act, not talk. A warrior does not sit back and wait for a fight. He goes out and confronts the danger."

Cyron shook his head. "Tyrel, maybe Marreanus is right. I want to keep Talia safe and fight as much as you, but maybe there is more to consider than the glory of battle?"

"What? You think walking in circles around the village will keep Talia safe? Is that what you think a warrior should be doing?"

Cyron lowered his head. "No, I don't know. Not really, but maybe these patrols are the best strategy. At least right now until we have a real plan to act on."

"A plan?" Yelled Tyrel. "I've got a plan for you. Find the Wolves. Kill the Wolves. That's the plan."

"That's no plan. That's just you being hot headed and impulsive like you were when we were colts. You can't run in swinging your sword and call that a plan. We don't even know for sure how many of them there are."

"That's just what I would expect from somebody like you."

"What is that supposed to mean?"

"If you were a real warrior, a real Centaur, you'd want to fight and not just talk like a...," he spit out the word "Human."

"A Human? I'm a Centaur." protested Cyron.

"Not in your heart," Tyrel said, pounding his chest. "Ever since that Human came here you've shown your true heart, your Human heart."

Cyron stared at Tyrel, not sure if this was the same someone he had known all his life. How could he say such a thing? Did he really know him at all?

"You keep walking in circles. I'm a warrior, not a guard dog. Maybe you can make peace with the Wolves like the Humans have. Or you can bark at them like a dog and then run and get Marreanus when they cross your path. I'm sure you two and your Human can talk your way out of it." Tyrel turned and galloped off. Cyron watched him vanish into the forest. He felt like he had been kicked in the chest. A swirl of anger and sorrow swam in his head.

Tyrel had been the first one to accept him when they were young colts. When the others had teased him, Tyrel stood up for him. He stood beside him and fought them alongside him. They had been inseparable friends ever since. Tyrel was his best friend, his brother. He and Tyrel had risked their lives side by side in many battles. They had depended on each other's trust and loyalty. Hearing Tyrel question whether he was a Centaur hurt him more than he could imagine.

Cyron didn't notice the half dozen Wolves surrounding him. When he caught the movement out of the corner of his eye, it was too late. The group rushed in before he could draw his blade. Two Wolves grabbed and held his arms while a third one jumped on his back lashing a rope around the neck. As he bucked and struggled, a fourth Wolf stepped in and slashed him with claws dripping with Cannullus' sleeping potion. Cyron flayed and kicked trying to free himself from his attackers. He cried out as they muzzled him and wrestled him to the ground. Ropes and nets were thrown over him, but still he struggled. Cyron weaken and felt dizzy. He shook his head trying to clear his mind and remain focused as the growing effects of the potion took hold. The Wolves pulled and yanked him about until the drug caused him to collapse into unconsciousness.

"Bind him tight," The leader growled.

"I'd like to rip out his heart," grunted another.

"We have orders to bring him back alive. But, Phalon never said anything about not hurting him a little…"

He kicked Cyron and snickered. The others joined in the fun and took their turns. The Wolves, using Cyron's knife, pinned a scroll to a tree. They lifted the unconscious Centaur and faded into the forest.

Behind a fallen tree a pair of terrified eyes grew teary. Hanar approached the tree and grabbed the blade releasing the scroll. "Poor Cyron. I've got to tell Talia. But, I can't go into the village. What am I going to do?" Hanar held his head and rocked back and forth. "What am I going to do?"

Talia swayed and grabbed the table to keep from falling. "What's wrong, child?" asked Ladena.

"I don't know. For a moment, I felt unsteady and dizzy. Like I was falling asleep." She faltered again.

"Come sit down," Said Ladena leading her to a seat.

"Cyron," her head jerked up. "Something's wrong with Cyron. Where is he?"

"Cyron is on patrol." Ladena said casually answering the question.

Panic filled Talia's voice. "He's in trouble, Ladena."

"Cyron is fine. He's with Tyrel." She laughed. "He's been in trouble ever since they met. Those two were always at the root of any mischief that happened in the village. They are like brothers and will always look after one another. Why, as young colts if you caught the right hand of one in the honey pot you could be sure to get the left hand of the other one as well."

She laughed again as the memories washed over her. "They are very capable young warriors. I'm sure things are fine." Ladena fixed her with a concerned stare. "This connection you have with your brother is new. It will take you time to manage and understand it. Don't over react when you feel his emotions. Cyron is a very passionate soul."

Talia reluctantly nodded. Her mind stilled, but her heart remained troubled. *Cyron, Cyron can you hear me. Cyron?* She closed her eyes and concentrated. *Cyron, Cyron,* Talia sighed and melted into her seat.

*L*adena rose and went to the door. Her eyes searched the darkness. "Whoever is there? Come out."

Talia came and stood beside her. "What is it?"

"We have a guest who will not show himself. Can you not feel him? Reach out as I shown you. Use your gift. Feel their presence."

Talia closed her eyes and emptied her mind. She reached out with her thoughts like probing hands feeling their way in the dark.

"Good" said Ladena. "Now push it out. Spread it around you. What do you feel?"

"I feel you and...there is something...someone. Yes, I feel him. He is close."

"Indeed," said Ladena. "Come out, you will not be harmed. Come out and state your intentions."

From behind the fence post a trembling figure stood up in the shadows.

"Hanar," shouted Talia. "What are you doing here?" Seeing the fright on his face she ran to him and put her arm around his shoulder.

"Hanar, are you all right?" He shook his head no.

"What's wrong?" He stared wide-eyed at Ladena. "You're safe here. There is nothing to be frightened of."

He never took his eyes off of the old Centaur who studied him with cautious interest.

"Come meet my grandmother." Talia said as she tried to calm the trembling Satyr. Grabbing his hand, she managed to pull the reluctant guest into the house.

"Hanar, this is my grandmother, Ladena." Hanar stood frozen, his eyes locked on Ladena.

"Ladena, I told you about Hanar."

"It appears I have frightened the speech out of him." Ladena said smiling.

"Hanar, you can relax. It's all right. I promise." Talia said.

He turned and faced Talia. Removing the Centaur from his view made him relax a bit. An eruption of words raced out of his mouth.

'I was hiding in the woods and I heard Cyron and Tyrel arguing and Tyrel got mad and ran off and the Wolves came and they attacked Cyron and they tied him up and they took him away and I couldn't do anything to help him and I told Cyron I heard the Wolves talking and we thought they wanted to capture you and instead they were after him all along and I had to tell you and I had to find you and I didn't know what to do and I had to come to the village and I was scared to come here and I found the house and I was afraid to come to the door and I was going to wait for you to come out."

Hanar's face scrunched into a ball. "Don't let them make me a slave." He closed his eyes and whimpered falling to his knee panting for breath.

Talia went to her knees in front of him. She grabbed his shoulder and shook him.

"Hanar, the Wolves captured Cyron?" He nodded yes not able to breath enough to speak. "When Hanar? When did this happen?"

"Just a little while ago," he said between pants. "Even though I was scared, I came straight here." He reached and pulled the knife and the scroll from his belt and handed them to Talia.

"They left this stuck to a tree."

"That's Cyron's blade," said Ladena, stepping forward and grabbing the blade, causing Hanar to rise and step back. "I gave it to him myself." She looked at the Satyr and smiled.

"You can calm yourself young Satyr. It was very brave of you to come here despite your fears. You are among friends here."

Talia grew pale as she read the scroll.

"What does it say, child?"

Talia's hands dropped to her side. "They have him and they want me to come or they will kill him." She shook her head. "I knew something was wrong. I felt it. I should have listened to my heart and acted. I felt his panic. I felt it."

"You can't go. They'll have you both and who knows what will happen then," cried Hanar.

"I have no choice. I've got to go or Cyron will die." Her eyes were wild with worry.

"He is right," Ladena added. "...to surrender yourself to the Wolves..."

"This is not the Wolves," Talia shouted out bitter words. "They are just tools. This message is written on the same kind of scroll they use at the castle. I see Thangor's and no doubt Cannullus' hands in this. Cyron said the Wolves and the Humans were working together. I guess he was right. The Wolves would just want to kill me, but Thangor wants to own me, to control me." She dropped the scroll and ran for the door.

"Hanar, stay here with Ladena."

Talia raced through the village. As she approached Marreanus' home, Tyrel stepped from the shadows and blocked her path. "What do you want here, Human?"

"I need to speak to Marreanus."

"You have nothing to say he would want to hear, so go back to your Human village and let us be?"

"Tyrel, I don't have time for this. Move or I will move you." Before he could touch the spear, he was reaching for, Talia threw a blast of energy at him that sent him flying across the yard and crashing into the wall of the house.

The noise brought Marreanus to the door. "What is going on here?" He saw his son lying sprawled against the wall and the angry faced young woman standing on his stoop.

"Is this how you treat those who have welcomed you into their community?"

"I asked him to move and he wouldn't." She said defiantly. "I don't have time for those who abandon their friends to be captured by their enemies."

"I do not understand," said Marreanus.

"Your son will explain. I need to know. Are you going to attack the Wolves?"

"I do not discuss our strategies and plans with outsiders. That is a private Centaur matter."

Somewhere between anger and worry Talia made her plea. "The Wolves have captured Cyron. Will you please help me get him back? We need to attack their village."

"Cyron captured? How? When?" Her eyes shot to Tyrel. "We do not have enough forces to take their village. It would be foolish to try. Besides, if they have Cyron he is already dead. The Wolves do not take prisoners."

"No, he is not. They are using him as a lure to bring me there. The Wolves are working with the castle."

"This we know. I cannot risk the fate of the whole village on one individual. We are warriors. Cyron understands the duty of sacrifice."

Talia's rage flashed. "It is too bad you do not understand the duty of loyalty and family." She turned and stomped away.

"Tyrel," Marreanus yelled turning on his son. "Weren't you on patrol with Cyron tonight?" The dazed young Centaur hung his head and nodded. "How did he get attacked and you did not?"

Tyrel's voice was hushed, just above a whisper. "We quarreled. He angered me and I left. I didn't know there were Wolfmen in the area. I never would have left him alone to face them if I knew. I...I..."

"You left your post? You abandoned one of your own?" Marreanus stared intently. "It appears you not only have a lot to learn about duty and honor, you have a lot to learn about a lot of things. There is nothing for you to be proud of this night, my son." He paused and sighed. "Nothing for either of us to be proud of."

Talia returned to Ladena's. "As soon as the sunrises I am going to the Wolfmen's village. They will be expecting me. Thangor knows that I will come."

"You must not do this. Cyron would not want you to do this. Do not be in such a hurry to be a sacrifice," pleaded the old Centaur.

"Ladena, grandmother," she said grasping her hands and forcing a smile. "I have dreamt of my family all my life. I have just found you. I will not let them harm my brother; not because of me. I must do this.

Once Cyron is free, I will find a way to get away from Thangor's clutches."

"There is a fog around you. I see no light to show you the path. I fear for you. Greedy hands are pulling at you."

"Don't, Talia," whispered Hanar. "Please."

"Stay with Ladena. She will take care of you."

"No, I am going with you," he insisted.

"Hanar, you cannot go. The scroll says that I must come alone. Besides, there is nothing you could do to help and the Wolfmen would surely kill you. Please stay here. I don't want to have to worry about you as well. I will be safe. Thangor wants me and my magic. I will not be harmed and he will not harm Cyron. I am too valuable and for now, so is Cyron. I have to trust that the thing he wants will also be the thing that will free me. Cyron is the one in danger. I cannot refuse."

Ladena and Hanar looked at each other and only fear and worry for Talia and Cyron remained between them.

CHAPTER 21

*A*t dawn, Talia headed east toward the Wolfmen's village. Thoughts of Thangor and Cannullus' smug faces powered her steps. She pounded her way through the brush, picturing each step as a strike against them. Her father's warnings of being controlled played over and over in her head. Once again magic seemed to have betrayed her. Once again, the thing she loved was causing pain to someone she loved. Once more her abilities were proving to be more a problem than an asset. Ever since her father began developing her talent, magic had been a pleasure. Not only did it allow her to spend time with her favorite person, but also magic made her feel special. It gave her a sense of belonging to something, of being a part of something. When the others rejected her, she still had her magic to comfort her and let her know that she was special. Now her magic had cost her a father, a brother, and soon her freedom. Magic had made her just something to be owned and used. Talia was beginning to feel her magic was a curse instead of a blessing.

Thoughts of killing Thangor and Cannullus entered her mind. Images of blasting them like the rock at the stone quarry. The idea troubled her. What was she becoming? Was magic doing this to her? Was this what she had to look forward to? Becoming something that frightened her. Having no more regard for life than Thangor or Cannullus. Could she really kill? Would she kill to save Cyron? To save herself? *Could I?* She asked herself. *I'm no killer, but I can't be Thangor's slave. Yes, I would.* She shuttered at the realization.

Once back at the castle what would happen? What of Cannullus? Would he use her secret to manipulate her? To coerce her, control her? What horrible things did they want her to do? What kind of monster would she become? How could she live with herself if she turned into someone like Cannullus? Talia never felt so confused.

"Talia," the sound of her name brought her out of the hole her heart had crawled in.

She looked up into the eyes of a contrite Tyrel.

"What are you doing here? Come to get your revenge?" she asked.

He hung his head in supplication. "No, I have come to ask for your pardon. If I had not abandoned Cyron he would not have been taken. I did not act honorably to him or to you. My actions were not worthy of a warrior. If you are going to the Wolfmen's village, I am offering my sword and my life to make thing right."

"An army of one?" she said exasperated. "Go home Tyrel. There is nothing for you here. If you are looking for a way to put your guilt to rest, I cannot help you." She walked around him and continued on without looking back.

Tyrel stood dejected. She was right; his guilt had brought him there. His pleas to his father to attack the Wolfmen and rescue Cyron had not made Marreanus change his mind. Offering his aid had been his only chance to regain his honor and dissuade his guilt. Since she had refused his help, there was no other way but to try and rescue Cyron on his own. He owed him that and he would not abandon his friend twice. Tyrel turned to head to the village. He found his path blocked by a Satyr.

"Do you wish to help?" asked Hanar, a mischievous smirk on his face.

"What? Who are you?"

"I am Hanar. Hanar Knoll. Talia and Cyron are my friends. I have been following her. I plan to find some way to help her rescue Cyron."

"You're the Satyr Cyron says hides in the woods near the village, aren't you?" Hanar nodded his head. "Why are you hiding and not with her?"

"She turned down my help just like she did you and left me with Ladena. I couldn't stay there knowing she was out here alone. I have been following her. I will follow her all the way to Wolfmen's village. I know I can help and I will. If you want to help we can work together. Maybe together we can do more."

'An army of two?" He raised a doubtful brow.

'It's twice as good as an army of one. Like my father said, "'Hanar it takes two legs to walk.'"

Tyrel thought for a moment studying the wide-eyed Satyr. "

Alright little Satyr. I can't go back to the village without Cyron. An army of two it is."

*C*yron opened his eyes and tried to stand. A wave of pain caused him to stop and wait for it to pass. His head was cloudy. It took some time before he remembered what had happened. Looking around, Cyron realized he was in an old storage shed. The floor was covered with strains of moldy straw and clumps of dirt. He walked around the room looking for a way out, but found the windows boarded, and the only way in or out was the door. The dank musty scent of the Wolves assaulted his nostrils.

"I'm in the Wolfmen's village. Why would they bring me here?" he wondered aloud. "The Wolves don't take prisoners. Why didn't they kill me? What could they want with me?" The warning Hanar had given him sprang to the front of his mind. *They're going to use me to get Talia.* The idea enraged him and he charged at the door.

Cyron kicked and beat at the door yelling, "You cowards. Come face me. I will not be held like a farm animal. Release me." The walls of the building shook, but would not give way.

He heard voices and movement outside. The door swung open. Half a dozen Wolves with swords and spears rushed in backing him into a corner. Phalon and Cannullus sauntered in behind them. One sniffing and snarling; the other smirking and sneering.

"So, you're Talia's brother? Twin brother, I believe. Yes, I can see the family resemblance. The same fiery emerald eyes. The same sanctimonious expression as your father." Cannullus said, waving a bony finger in disapproval.

"Your name is Cyron, I understand. I am Cannullus. It is a pleasure to meet you. I hope you will forgive the unorthodox method we used to get you here, but your assistance is required." A sarcastic smile crossed his lips.

"You can forget about using me for bait. Talia will never come," said a defiant Cyron. Hatred hung on every word.

"You don't know your sister very well. Do you? Oh yes, that's right, you just met her." Cannullus snickered.

"Well, I have known her all her life. There is no doubt that the head strong little..." He paused "...dear, is already on the way. And who knows, maybe your mother as well."

"You are my guest," interjected Phalon. "I am Phalon, leader of the pack." He feigned a bow. "I hope that you approve of your accommodations?" He swept the room with a gesture and laughed. The other Wolves yelped.

Smoldering with rage, it took all the strength Cyron could muster to remain silent and in control. *Hold your temper. Stay in control,* he kept telling himself. *Your moment will come.* Cyron did not doubt Cannullus' words. He hadn't known Talia very long, but he had no doubt that she was on her way. Something deep in the back of his mind felt her getting closer. He knew she would be there soon. *They don't know about Cyrenia. There may be an advantage in that,* he thought. *Stay in control. Your moment will come.*

"What do you want us to do with him? Should we make him sleep again?" asked Phalon.

"No, just keep an eye on him until all the players arrive. I want Talia to see that he is alive and unhurt." He added as a warning staring at Cyron. "At least for now..."

Cannullus turned and exited the building, followed by Phalon and his horde.

Cyron fell back on his haunches in frustration. *How am I going to get out of here? How can I stop Talia from coming?* He let out a long frustrated breath. *What will they do to us once they have us both?* The questions whirled through his mind. Being a warrior, action had always been the answer, but it was obvious to him that he would have to think his way out of this.

Talia proceeded to the village unaware of the angry yellow eyes that tracked her progress. The Wolves had been told to watch for her, but not impede her arrival. They had picked up her presence from the moment she entered the woods and had sent word to Phalon she was on the way. Talia let her sense of Cyron guide her steps. The thought of other dangers never crossed her mind. She didn't notice the poisonous striped viper she almost stepped on, nor the pit of sinking sand she barely skirted. Her magic reacted to her state of mind, obliterating anything that interfered with her goal, unconsciously shielding her from harm. Her only thoughts were for Cyron and the things she may have to do to gain his freedom.

The idea of going back to the castle and being Thangor's wife angered her one moment and saddened her the next. A thousand scenarios ran through her mind, but none solved her problems. None were any more satisfying than the one before it. To surrender herself would free Cyron and leave her Thangor's puppet. To refuse would cause Cyron to be killed. To fight could get both of them killed. Each step, each thought, caused her to give in to the reality of it.

Talia sensed Cyron more clearly. The feeling grew with each step she took. The intensity of his emotions, the force of his anger made her worry about him even more. *He's alive.* She tried to comfort her self with the thought.

The Wolves didn't realize that while they were tracking, they were being tracked. Two pairs of well-hidden eyes were stealthily trailing them. Hanar and Tyrel were keeping pace, but being careful to remain down wind and out of sight.

"Have you any idea what we're going to do?" Hanar asked.

Tyrel gave him a sly grin. "Die honorably as warriors."

Hanar gave him a sharp glare. "Not funny," he said.

CHAPTER 22

*P*rince Thangor, accompanied by a half dozen of his most trusted guards, approached the village. Thangor was adorned in his most ostentatious uniform. It was a strawberry red suit with black strips down the arms and legs, tall shiny black boots, a chest full of ribbons and metals, epaulets with gold rope and a matching red hat, complete with a foot-high black feather. The feather had broken in the wind and now flopped into his face causing him to constantly brush it away. The guards found this humorous, but dared not let Thangor see their amusement.

Thangor's horse, a handsome muscular Friesian with a glossy black coat, was duly adorned with a braided red saddle and so much headgear the animal could barely see. The horse constantly tossed his head to remove the tassels from his eyes. It looked as though the horse was mimicking the actions of his rider. This amused the guards as well.

The parade trotted into the village as members of the pack studied them from behind buildings and trees. The village was a large collection of rundown shacks, lean-tos, and shanties made of rotting boards and scrap metal. There were broken windows, damaged shutters, and decaying thatched roofs with holes in them. The ground was heavily matted with clumps of weeds and dead shrubberies. Broken mining equipment, discarded pieces of furniture, and piles of debris lay scattered all over the ground. The air smelled of waste and decay.

The area had been abandoned by miners who had given up the excavating of silver once the vein in the nearby mine had petered out. No attempts had been made as of yet to repair or clean up the place. It remained a deserted and dilapidated settlement waiting for the forest to reclaim it. Instead, the Wolf pack had claimed it as their own.

When their numbers had grown to require more space, the Wolves moved from the caves that had been their home. Taking over the abandoned mining town was a declaration from the pack that they had become a force once again; a force determined to reclaim their lost status. Phalon intended to make his pack the ruling power in the land. His vision was for this to be the start of a future kingdom.

Thangor and his company rode up to Cannullus and Phalon waiting outside the largest structure of the village. Throwing his leg over and sliding off the horse, Thangor looked like a child dismounting his rocking horse. He looked around with an expression of total disgust on his face. Placing a scented kerchief to his nose, he immediately made his intentions known.

"Cannullus, let us conclude our business quickly. I have no intentions of spending a night here." He looked around with narrowed eyes emphasizing his disapproval. Thangor started brushing his clothes as if the proximity to the place made him dirty.

"I will have to bathe for a week" he protested.

"We have the boy." Cannullus said. ignoring his discomfort. "Talia has not yet arrived."

"She's on the way," interjected Phalon. "My pack brothers have been tracking her progress. She's not far away." He bared a toothy grin.

"I wish to welcome you, Prince Thangor." He offered a bow.

Thangor eyed him briefly, dismissing his presence and turning back to Cannullus.

"Good. The less time I spend here the better. We have ridden for two days and all last night to get here. Is there somewhere I might be able to lounge? Somewhere that has been recently serviced," he added.

"We have prepared a place for you." Phalon rushed to the door, pointing the way.

"This? This is the best you have?" Thangor eyes were wide with astonishment. He looked to Cannullus.

"They are very," Cannullus dragged out the word, "...rural."

Thangor looked inside the door and retreated back to the front of the building. Red faced he shouted. "There will be no waiting. Get her here. Now!" He stammered pointing at the horsemen. "Send the horses."

Cannullus hurriedly spoke to Lucius, the captain of the guards, and they galloped off. The contrary trio re-entered the building, with Thangor complaining the entire time. He brought the scented kerchief back to his nose.

*T*alia found a spread of moss under an oak tree and sat to rest. Removing her shoes, she rubbed her feet. Leaning back against the trunk, she allowed herself a moment of peace until the howling calls of Wolves broke her relaxation. Their calls echoed eerily throughout the forest. One would call, another would answer, and so on until the calls came dangerously close. The noise was coming from everywhere around her. Talia searched for the source of the calls. They were near. She could feel them, but not yet see them.

Slipping into her shoes, Talia stood. For the first time since leaving Ladena's house, something other than anger and frustration gripped her. For the first time, she began to fear for her own safety. If she were harmed or killed, what would happen to Cyron? Where were the Wolves? What did these calls mean?

The savage faces of the pack began to appear from behind trees and bushes. Angry and jaundiced eyes peered at her. Talia's heart began to race. The Wolves bared their sharp fangs and growled a low throaty grumble.

"I am going to the village as the scroll ordered!" She shouted, her magic gathering in the back of her mind. Her fingers twitched as the energy tickled her hands. The Wolves moved in closer. Talia braced herself, preparing to release a barrage of magic she hoped would cause them to back away.

The forest grew still and silent. The distant sound of hooves broke the standoff. At first Talia's heart rose with excitement. She thought the Centaurs had come to fight.

But then she realized the sound was coming from in front of her, not from behind her. Her heart settled in her throat. What was this? The prince's guards appeared, weaving their way around trees and through the foliage. They halted in front of her.

"Clear the path. Give us room." Lucius ordered. The Wolves complied and move aside.

"The prince awaits your arrival," Lucius offered her the reins to the prince's horse. Talia relaxed and took a deep breath. Unnerved by the number of Wolves surrounding her, she quickly ascended the horse. They turned and started back to the village with the pack trailing behind.

"The Humans are ordering the Wolves around," whispered Hanar. "This is bad, very bad. We have two foes to deal with."

"Didn't you know this?" Tyrel asked surprised by his statement. "We've got to get back to the village. This will convince Marreanus to attack. I'm sure of it."

"You can go back, but I'm not going anywhere without Talia and Cyron."

"We can't fight the Wolves and the Humans."

"There's more than one way to solve problems. You don't always have to fight."

"What do you have in mind little Satyr? Do you know magic or something as good?"

"I don't know, but something will come up. My father always said so. 'Hanar, there's more than one path in the forest.'" Tyrel looked to the sky and shook his head.

*T*alia entered the rickety building and stood before a smirking Thangor. He was seated with Cannullus and Phalon flanking him on both sides. "Where is Cyron?" she demanded.

Thangor smiled, held up a finger, and tilted his head as if he were waiting to hear something. Talia drew in her anger and relented.

"Please, Thangor," she said through clenched teeth. Thangor raised a brow, cupped one hand and made an open and closing motion signaling he wanted more.

"Please, Thangor ..." up went his hand and then a nod. Talia started again. "Please, your highness, may I see Cyron?"

"Better," he said. "But we will still have to work on your delivery. I didn't quite believe you felt the sincerity in your heart. You didn't have an apologetic enough tenor."

He laughed at the dejected expression on her face. Snapping his fingers, he said, "Take her to see her dear beloved brother. Give them a few moments alone together and then bring her back here. We have some arrangements to make before I leave this..." He looked around. "...this enchanting retreat."

Approaching the building, Cyron and Talia felt each other as if they were standing side by side. Their anger and sadness merged like two rivers pouring into a delta. They embraced when she came into the room.

"Are you all right? Did they hurt you?"

"I'm fine. You shouldn't have come. Now they control both of us. No matter what they say, don't agree to it. You have to get away from here."

"I can't, Cyron. They will kill you if I don't agree to go with them willingly."

"As the oldest, I am telling you to do as I say and get out of here."

"Who says you're the oldest? Don't think that you can order me around. I came to save you and I'm going to do it whether you like it or not."

"Of course, I'm the oldest. Don't be silly. Males are always the oldest." They glared at each other as only brother and sister can. Cyron broke the silence.

"This is not the time for this. Just do as I say and get out of here."

Talia bristled at the comments. The sound of the Wolves outside the door brought her back to the situation at hand.

"Cyron, I know Thangor. He needs to feel he's in control. All I have to do is agree to what he wants. He'll let you go and then I can figure out a way to escape from the castle. I did it once; I'll do it again. I'll be back in the village in no time. Please do this my way. If you don't, none of us may get out of this alive. Besides, there are things you don't know. I can't fight them right now."

"Talia, I'm a Centaur, a warrior. I can't let you sacrifice yourself for me. I have my honor. A warrior fights or dies."

Tears crested the corners of Talia's eyes.

"Please, I just found you, brother. I can't lose you. Please don't die." She fell into his arms weeping. Cyron pulled her close, laying his head on her shoulder.

The door burst open and the Wolves ordered her out. "Alright," said Cyron wiping her tears. "But, I'm coming for you, soon."

"You won't have to," she said as she left.

CHAPTER 23

*C*yron's in there," whispered Tyrel. Hanar nodded his agreement. There are only four guards. If we can quietly kill them, then we can get him out of there. We have to be quick and silent so they don't sound the alarm."

"Kill them?" said a startled Hanar, leaning away and shaking his head. "I've never killed anything in my life. I can't kill. Not even one of them. I can't."

Tyrel looked at him as if he had just punched him in the face. "What did you think we were going to do? Talk them into letting him go? Of course, we have to kill them. If we don't kill them, they'll kill him and us."

"But...but...," said a reluctant Hanar.

"Here," Tyrel said shoving a dagger into his hand. "Stay here, cower behind these bushes and protect yourself. I'll do this myself."

Tyrel gave him a look of disgust before disappearing into the brush. Hanar held out the blade and stared at it. He closed his finger around the handle and quickly unclenched it as if the knife were a hot coal. Hanar thought of Cyron and closed his hand, quickly opening it again. He thought of Talia and repeated the act. He thought of his parents and closed his hand, but did not open them this time. A mixture of anger and sorrow welled up in him and he rose from his hiding place.

Tyrel positioned himself behind one of the Wolves and impaled him with his sword quickly pulling his dead body into the bushes and out of view. He crept along the back of the building and took aim with his bow and arrow, bringing down a second of the guards. Rolling the body out of sight, he noticed that the third and fourth guards were in eyesight of each other. If he brought down one, the other would see it and be free to sound the alarm.

Deciding that there was no other option, he rushed the nearest Wolf and struck him a deathblow with his sword. Immediately, he drew his bow and without thinking or aiming he fired an arrow at the last of the Wolves, hoping to bring him down before he could signal for help. The arrow whizzed past the head of a trembling Hanar. He stood over the body of the last guard with the blade protruding from his back. He never noticed the arrow or how close the Centaur had come to killing him. Tyrel was amazed and relieved. He rushed to the body, grabbed the feet and dragged it behind a tree, sweeping up leaves to cover it.

"Good job, Hanar." Tyrel said when he returned. "I was sure they had me. I'm not nearly as good with a bow as Cyron. He would have made that shot easily." He saw the Satyr still standing there, looking at the ground where the body of the dead Wolfman had laid. A single tear rolled down his cheek.

Tyrel grabbed his hand and pulled him to the door of the building. He forced open the door and whispered inside, "Cyron, get your hooves out here." Cyron appeared out of a dark corner. Before he could say a word, Tyrel said, "We don't have time for explanations. Just come on, we have to get away from here."

Cyron rushed to his friend and they locked arms saying more with a look than words could say. Looking around he asked. "Where's Talia? We can't leave without her."

"She's gone back to the main building. Come on, we'll get away from here and figure out how to rescue her. Hurry up." he whispered, walking away and dragging a despondent Hanar behind him. Cyron reluctantly followed as they disappeared into the underbrush, being careful not to leave a trail that could be followed.

"Hanar, are you alright?" Cyron asked the blank faced Satyr. "What's wrong with him?"

"He killed one of the Wolves. It was the first time he had ever killed anything. I didn't believe he would do it, but he did. If he hadn't that last Wolf would have sounded the alarm and we'd be in a fight for our lives."

'Poor guy. He's no warrior. He's not built for this kind of thing. Why did you bring him?"

"I didn't." Tyrel protested. He found me on the trail. We were both following Talia. She left him with Ladena. She and I...well she wouldn't let anyone come with her. That Human of yours is stubborn."

"She's not my Human. She's my sister. She may only be part Centaur, but she's braver than any Centaur I know," snapped Cyron.

"You're right, I sorry. I was wrong about her. She does have a noble heart." He lowered his head and his voice. "I didn't mean to leave you to the Wolves. I know it's no excuse, but I was so upset about my father not doing anything about the Wolves. I lost my temper."

"We have to think about getting Talia back now. They'll be plenty of time for that later." He turned to the torpid Satyr.

"Hanar, are you going to be alright? We still need you. Talia still needs you."

His voice was just above a whisper. "I thought about my father and my mother and how I couldn't help them, and what the Wolves did to them. It made me angry and I wanted to..." His voice trailed off. Tears began falling from his eyes. Hanar swallowed and raised his chin.

"I'll be all right. I'll do whatever has to be done to help Talia." He wiped his eyes with the back of his hands and looked at the two Centaurs with a sad, lost stare as if all the emotion had been wrung out of him. "Let's go," he said.

CHAPTER 24

I hope that your reunion was a pleasant one. You can see that he is safe and unharmed and will remain that way as long as you cooperate," Thangor said with a satisfied grin. "I told you that if I had to, I would come and retrieve you. Maybe now you will understand that your fate is indelibly tied to mine and is in my hands."

Talia stood stone-faced before him. She did not hear him. Her mind was with Cyron. She knew he was free, she felt it. The feeling was unmistakable. Somehow, he was moving away from her. She could feel he was excited, but worried. The thought of Cyron being free was thrilling, but saddening. Talia was glad for his escape, but wished it had come before she had surrendered herself into Thangor's power.

Despite her apprehension, she managed a small smile. Thangor missed the smile, but not by the suspicious eyes of Cannullus, who narrowed his eyes and stared at her as if he was trying to read her mind.

"We will be leaving for the castle within the hour. I have to get my soon-to-be bride back to the safety of our walls."

"What about Cyron?" Talia asked. "When will you set him free? You have no reason to hold him now that I have given myself over to you."

"He will remain here a guest of Phalon and his pack. Once we are away from here and you are safely ensconced in the castle, he will be set free and allowed to return to his home, but for now we will hold him to make sure that your cooperation is complete."

"I have your word on this?" she asked.

"Talia, you wound me with your suspicions. Of course, it will be as I say. I am the future king, am I not? My word is law." His smile was unpleasant and his tone was dripping with sarcasm.

"What about our payment?" Phalon asked feeling as though his participation was being over looked. "There were promises made."

"Yes, yes," said Thangor giving the comments the smallest of concerns. "Cannullus will remain behind and handle things. As it is, we will have to ride for many hours to reach suitable accommodations in which to spend the night."

Thangor rose and approached Talia with an air of superiority. He looped his arm around her waist and pulled her out the door with him.

"You are sure the boy is secure?" asked Cannullus turning to Phalon.

"He is still locked away. When do we kill him?"

"We will save that happy task for later. First, I wish to question him. There may be things he can tell us that will aid in our elimination of the Centaurs."

"Then we rip out his heart."

"After I have spoken with him, you may do whatever you wish with him." They followed Thangor out the door.

Talia cooperated without resistance. She could feel Cyron. He was near and he was agitated. She could feel his eyes on her. Talia resisted looking around for fear she would see him and give his position away. *Just wait,* she thought. *Just wait.*

Cyron felt her caution. Then he heard, *Just wait.* The sound of the words made him snap his head erect. *Talia,* he thought. *Yes, just wait.* It was her. *I will,* he mouthed the words as he thought them.

"You will ride with me, my dear." Thangor whispered in her ear. "I am not letting you out of my sight or my reach again."

He turned to the Wizard. "Take care of this situation Cannullus, and meet us in Alserra. The manor of Lord Jannus will do for a night." He looked around. "At least it is clean. Make haste, we have a wedding to plan." Thangor beamed with satisfaction as he, Talia, and his guards galloped out of the village.

"Hanar, hop on my back" said Cyron. "You'll never be able to keep up with their horses." Keeping to the high foliage, the trio followed closely behind.

"*I* wish to question the boy," Cannullus said, moving to the makeshift prison. He extracted a small bottle containing a familiar blue liquid. "I'll have no problem finding out all that I wish to know." A callous smirk appeared on his face.

"The guards? The door?" Phalon shouted as they approached the enclosure. He leapt into the room. Looking around, he pounded his fist against the walls.

"Fools, fools." He turned to Cannullus. "He can't have gotten far. We will find him."

Cannullus erupted with rage. "You idiot! Now everything is in jeopardy. If Thangor finds out about this, I could lose all that I have planned. What made me think I could depend on you and your worthless mutants? Gather your wretched dogs and find him."

Phalon stepped back. The source of his anger shifted. He snarled, swiping at Cannullus with clawed hands ripping long tears in Cannullus' robe. Bleeding scratches ran down his chest. Cannullus screamed and fell back in shock. "I told you before, we are not your underlings. This is our domain. You will not order us around like your slaves. You will not speak to us like that."

Murderous eyes bore down on him. Baring deadly fangs, they encircled Cannullus, bearing down on him. The group began to elicit throaty growls.

Cannullus quickly realized the error of his outburst. "I seem to have gotten overly emotional. It is just that we are so close to accomplishing our goal..." his shaky voice trailed off as he fumbled for words.

"Phalon," he said in a softer pleasant voice. He raised one hand in submission while searching in his pocket with the other. "Don't be rash and jeopardize our plans. I spoke without thinking; from my emotions, not my head. You can't expect me not to be upset by this occurrence." Cannullus retrieved a vial of reddish liquid. With one swift motion, he turned in a circle throwing the vial to the ground. A crimson cloud erupted quickly, engulfing the advancing horde of claws and teeth.

Cannullus, with the hem of his robe to his nose and mouth agilely moved through the smoke. Phalon and his pack fell to their knees coughing, holding their throats and rubbing their eye. Cannullus dashed to his horse, hopped on, and raced off toward Alserra.

As the cloud of gas slowly dissipated, Phalon rose to his feet and howled with frustration. "I'll rip out his beating heart and eat it before his dying eyes." Phalon coughed and shouted at those around him. "Gather the pack. Forget about the boy, he will be dealt with when we take care of the other Centaurs. We need to capture the Witch. Meet me in Alserra. We will put an end to this partnership and take our revenge."

"What of you?" one of the group asked.

"I am coming, but first I must gather up the means of our revenge. Go now. They will be at the big house, the Lord's manor."

ybela!" Phalon shouted. She appeared at the mouth of the cave as if she were made of mist. "The time is now, Cybela. We need to act before they return to the castle. Once they are there, Cannullus will raise all of Mandoria against us. We must get the Witch under our control, now. I have seen the envy in Cannullus' eyes. I know she is the key. Her magic is the answer to our needs."

"Quiet yourself, Phalon. I have devised a way." A salacious grin crossed her face. "Get me close to her without interference. I will perform a melding. It will allow me to join with her. Once I trap her inside her own mind, I will have control of her body and her power."

"This is possible?"

"Yes, Phalon. She is young, inexperienced. I am sure I can subdue her will."

Phalon's smile out grew his face. "Come then, we must meet with the rest of the pack. Tonight, we strike. Tomorrow, we rule."

Cybela disappeared back into the cave, reemerging moments later with a red pouch clattering with glass vials hanging from her shoulder.

Moving with the speed of feral beasts, they wove a path through the forest, sometimes on two legs and sometimes on four. Cybela chanted incantations and offered prayers. She stopped often, marking symbols of magic on her body and drinking one of the many vials of colored liquid. She tossed silver colored flakes into the air and let them rain down on her, pressing and rubbing them into her body until she was coated in them.

With every shower of the silver flakes, her features grew fainter and less recognizable, becoming eerily translucent in the process. Her form, like smoke, morphed and twisted from Cybela the Shaman into a tree, a bush, a raven; to whatever thing her concentration fell upon.

Along the path to Alserra, they began to encounter members of the pack. They gasped and pulled back in fear as they saw the Shaman shifting and altering herself into the shape and form of different things.

"They have settled into the manor," one of the pack said.

"Has Cannullus arrived?" asked Phalon.

"He rode in a short time ago. After he came, the guards came out of the manor and began patrolling the grounds."

"That will mean they are expecting us. It does not matter. If we have to kill them all and take the Witch, we will."

"What is going on?" asked Hanar. "It looks like the whole pack is gathering here."

"I don't know. We better be careful. I don't want them to know we're here." Cyron shifted in their perch behind a thicket of trees.

"We have to find a better spot to keep an eye on things," said Tyrel. "There are too many of them. We wouldn't have a chance if they discover us."

"What about that cliff?" Hanar pointed to a small plateau jetting out of the hillside.

"Good eye, Hanar. From up there we can see what's going on all around us and avoid being detected." Cyron nodded. "I'm glad you're back with us. I was worried about you."

Hanar fumbled with a twig. "I've never killed anything before. I didn't know if I could do it. But, I couldn't let them hurt you or Talia or Tyrel, so I did what I had to do."

"You did good," Tyrel offered. "There was no way I could have gotten this far without you."

"Like my father used to say, 'Hanar, you never know what you can do until you've done it.' I'm just not sure that killing is what he was talking about." The trio moved back and circled around the gathered horde of Wolfmen and made their way to the plateau.

"That father of yours had a saying for all situations, didn't he?" Tyrel asked.

"My father was very wise."

"What is it, Cyron?" Tyrel asked.

"There," he pointed to the manor. "...on the second floor in the corner. It's Talia."

"How do you know it's her?"

"It's her. I can feel her. She is safe for now. I can sort of hear her." He twisted his head straining to hear. "I'm sure she knows we're here." Cyron closed his eyes and pictured her face. *I will not leave you. I will find a way to rescue you. I promise.*

I know, came the response.

"When we return to the castle, we'll have to gather our forces and return to deal with Phalon," Thangor said. "I'm afraid you've made a mess of things, Cannullus. All you had to do was promise him anything. It did not matter if we honored your promise or not. After all you are not the ruler of Mandoria. You're just a..."

"Servant," grumbled Cannullus.

"No, I was going to say subject, Wizard." Thangor scowled at him. "Now thanks to your lack of tact we will have to deal with both the Centaurs and the Wolfmen ourselves."

"I did not believe Phalon would reveal his treachery so soon. I have always suspected he had hidden plans, but I thought we would be rid of the Centaurs before he would show his hand. After all, they are a threat to the Wolfmen and only a nuisance to us."

"Your excuses will not cover your mistakes. Phalon was your suggestion and your responsibility. I do not accept you leaving your messes for me to set right."

"I beg your forgiveness, my lord." Cannullus offered through clenched teeth. "I sought only to serve the crown. If that vile creature did as he was told, all things would have ended more favorably."

"The only good thing that has come out of this misadventure is that we have Talia back. I want you to make sure that she is guarded day and night. I don't care if you have to do it yourself."

"She is secured in one of the bedrooms. There is a guard at the door. He has orders not to allow anyone to enter or leave that room. I shall personally check in on her." Cannullus twitched his fingers. *"We have much to discuss, Talia and I."*

Thangor brushed at his clothing. "Between the Wolfmen's village and hours upon hours on that beast, I need the soothing relaxation of a hot bath and a soft bed. It will take a month of ablutions to remove the memory of their stench from my body," swiping his perfumed handkerchief across his nose.

"Cannullus, see that my bath is prepared." he said, fanning the air with his kerchief. "I am in utter misery."

Cannullus bowed as he headed for the door.

"...and find yourself something proper to wear. I would not believe that thing you wear could look any worse. They may have some old potato sacks lying around that you can fashion yourself another of those god-awful robes," he added, reclining on a chaise like an old woman with the vapors.

Cannullus stormed up the stairs, angry that he was expected to perform the duties of a lowly valet.

"Open the door." He barked at the soldier guarding Talia's room. He entered and slammed the door shut. Talia turned from the window to meet him.

"We have a few things to settle before we return to the castle. Regardless of your new position with the royal family, we need an understanding between us."

Moving forward, he towered over her. Talia kept her chin raised and tried to hide the fear creeping into her eyes.

Cannullus began to pace about the room, moving back and forth like a cat stalking a mouse. "Your secret shame is safe with me, but I don't think that it is unreasonable for me to expect a favor or two in return."

"What kind of favors could you expect from me? I will be a prisoner. There is no power in the dungeons."

"Come now, my dear. You know that your prison, as you call it, will not be some dark soggy hole. Instead you will have a suite of silks and furs, and chains of pearls and gems. I think that your sufferings will be bearable."

"A prison is still a prison. It does not matter what it is made of, the purpose and the results are the same."

"I see that your father's philosophy has indeed been engrained in you. Let us hope that you also have his good sense. Our little secret will remain just that, our little secret, if you are willing to be as generous with me as I have been with you. It is up to you."

"What if I tell Thangor? What if I confess and throw myself on his mercy? That would end our agreement, and maybe end you as well."

"So, our little she-cat has decided to show her claws." Cannullus sat on the bed and smiled. "What about your newly-found family? Have you confessed to them? Have you revealed your crime? Do they know that you killed your father? That you ran from the castle to escape discovery and punishment? Does your dear brother realize that his sweet innocent sister has been lying to him since he met her?"

Talia drew back covering her face with her hands. Cannullus rose and stood before her. "I didn't think so. Young Sorceress, I think it is time that you realize who you are beholden to. When we return to the castle, I will expect our alliance to be mutually beneficial. I will keep your secrets and you will aid me now and then when I require it. Is that understood?"

Talia stood paralyzed, holding herself and fighting back tears.

"Is that understood?" His voice rose in tone and strength. Talia nodded. "Say it!" he demanded.

"Yes. I understand." Tears trickled down her cheek.

"Good. I am sure we will become one happy castle now that we understand each other."

Cannullus smirked and left the room. Talia buried her face into the bed muffling her sobs.

CHAPTER 26

*W*et and wobbly from a bath and two bottles of wine, Thangor arrived at Talia's door swaying unsteadily. "Lock the door once I'm in." He told the guard. "No matter what you hear don't let anyone in. Do you understand me?"

"Yes, my lord."

"No one," he repeated placing a finger to his lips as he hic-upped and closed the door. The room was lit only by the moonlight that filtered through the windows. Thangor gathered his robe around himself and stumbled to the bed, plopping down beside the sleeping Talia. He leaned over and stroked her hair.

"I do care about you Talia. I don't want you only for your powers. As children, we promised ourselves to each other. I meant it. I still mean it. My life would be so hollow without you." He leaned in and kissed her cheek.

Talia stirred opening her eyes. She drew herself into a ball pulling away from him. "Thangor, what are you doing here? What do you want?"

"I want you, Talia. I've always wanted you. I want you to be my queen and to rule beside me."

"You want my gift. That is what you really want. To control it. You do not care about me. You don't care about anything. If Cannullus had my gift you would toss me aside like ashes."

"No, Talia. I have always wanted you. I want us to be like we were when we were children. Cannullus is nothing." He crunched up his face as if he smelled something disagreeable. "Cannullus is a scheming viper."

'That's the wine talking. You stink of it. Tomorrow when your mind is clear, you and your court Wizard will go back to your seedy partnership."

"I work with him. I have to. You have to have allies to survive in the court. You don't know how much influence he has. My father trusts him implicitly." He pulled his face into a frown. "But I know better. I'm not as vapid as he thinks I am. I see his scheming and plotting. I'll gladly get rid of him if that will please you. We don't need him." Thangor ground the heel of his palm into his eye. "Besides after what he has done I know you don't want him around."

"Done? What has he done, Thangor?"

"Your father, they fought so long for the position of court magician. Cannullus knew he could never match your father's abilities so he had to get rid of him somehow. He tried for years to discredit him, but your father was too clever, too powerful for him. If your father had not been injured, Cannullus would never have been able to press his advantage." He yawned. "I did not know until the deed was done."

"What deed? What did Cannullus do?"

"Until after his death. After he had poisoned him..."

"Poisoned him?" she screamed. "Cannullus poisoned my father? But...but how?" Her heart pounded threatening to beat out of her chest.

"When your father was recovering from his injuries, he switched the medicine he was taking for something else. Cannullus is an Alchemist. He knows all about poisons."

Eyes she thought exhausted of tears found a new source. "Why didn't you tell me? Why didn't you do something about it?"

Thangor stood shocked by her ferocity. "Court politics," he mumbled casually. "I learned a long time ago that you protect yourself. There are always those who would do you harm in order to take your place. It's the way things are done. Talleon would understand."

He wobbled and held his head in his hands. He laughed. "He thinks I don't know." Thangor winked and tapped the side of his head. "I have my spies too. I'm not as frivolous as people think."

Talia leapt to her feet, crashing into him. "All this time you let him make me believe I had killed my father. That my magic had been the reason for his death. That I caused the injuries that killed him."

"I'm sorry Talia," He hung his head. "I should have said something. Done something, but..."

"But you just thought of what you wanted. You let that monster kill my father. You let me believe I was responsible so you and he could control me."

She pounded his chest with clenched fist. "You let me suffer with that guilt. I hate you. Hate you."

Thangor wrapped his arms around her and held her struggling body tight to his as she dissolved in a wet rag. "I'm sorry, Talia. I'm sorry." His words were slurred, but sincere.

"The Witch. Where is she?" Phalon demanded.

"The second floor." One of his pack members pointed. "The corner room. We saw her in the window."

"Where is Cybela? Cybela?"

"I am here Phalon," came the answer from a sneering young Wolfman.

"What is this?" The group pulled away. Apprehension and fright on their faces.

"Have no fear. I will continue to change and alter until I meld with the chosen one." She morphed again into a younger version of herself. "I will need some distraction so that I can get near to her."

"We will attack at the front of the house." Phalon said, his eyes jetting about as he created plans. "All of their attention will be on the attack. Can you climb that vine and reach the window?"

"Yes," Cybela replied, turning her answer into a smile. "Just make sure that you keep them busy until I have done what needs to be done.

You will know that it is complete when I appear at the front of the house."

"How will I know it is you?"

"You will know," She winked and laughed.

"Let us strike now." Phalon moved from the shelter in the tree line surrounding the manor and headed for the house. Reaching deep within himself, he let out the most blood-curdling howl he could produce. The rest of the pack began to join in. Soon there was a chorus of wild yelps and howls echoing through the woods. The sound was loud and frightening.

Cybela joined the parade of bodies. She broke off from the other as they neared the house. Hiding in the shadows of shrubbery and trees around the house, she made her way to the rear of the building. Placing her dagger between her teeth, she freed her hands for climbing. With cat like reflexes Cybela scaled the vines making her way to Talia's window.

"What is going on?" Hanar asked.

"It looks like the Wolfmen are going to attack the manor." Tyrel said.

"But, why? I thought they were allies?" Hanar asked.

"I don't know. Maybe that's why we saw Cannullus ride in like dragons were chasing him. He did look like he had been in a fight. The allies seem to have become enemies." Tyrel said, looking from Cyron to Hanar searching for agreement. "What do you think?" he asked Cyron with a poke to the shoulder.

Cyron had his eyes closed. His face balled up as if he was in pain. Tyrel shook him again.

"Cyron, what's wrong."

Cyron opened his eyes. They were full of pain. He laid a hand to his chest. "It's Talia. I don't know what wrong, but she's hurting."

"They're torturing her." Hanar yelled.

"No," said Cyron. "She's not in physical pain. It's her heart. Something has hurt her." He held the bridge of his nose. "I can feel it. She is very sad."

"We've got to get her out of there. Right now." The Satyr said and headed down the cliff.

"Come on!" yelled Tyrel as he followed. "We can use the Wolf attack as cover."

Cyron closed his eyes and concentrated. *We're coming Talia. Hang on, I will be there soon."*

"It's the Wolf pack. They're massing in the front of the house," Lucius, the Captain of the Guards, reported to Cannullus.

"Where is the Prince?" asked Cannullus.

"He is safe in his quarters."

"And the girl?"

"Still locked in her room." Lucius answered.

"Good. No use in bothering the Prince with this, we will handle Phalon and his horde. Gather all the manor guards and staff. Arm them and join us at the main entrance. We'll teach them who's in charge and send them skulking back into the woods."

Cannullus stepped to the front of the cluster of guards. With the addition of the manor guards and the household staff his army had grown significantly in size.

Swords drawn and bows quilled, they formed a shield before the manor. With Phalon at the head of the pack, they marched to face the men, claws and fangs bared and hungry.

"You left so soon!" Phalon yelled to Cannullus. "Our affairs were not yet settled."

"The court does not appreciate one of its members being attacked. If you behave like animals, then we will treat you as such."

"Does this mean that our alliance is at an end?" His gravelly voice was taunting and smug.

"You have lost our trust so there can be no alliance without trust. Go back to your lands and we will leave you in peace. Come any further and it is war. A war you cannot win."

"We shall see about that," Phalon raised his claw. "Attack!"

A massive line of Wolfmen raced forward from behind Phalon, howls and growls spurring them on. A wall of arrows sailed out to meet them, halting most of the attackers. They regrouped and another line rushed forward only to meet the same fate.

Wolfmen laid piled on top of each other pin-cushioned with arrows. Those who survived the arrows and made it near the house were slashed by swords or skewered by spears. Armed men rushed forward and severed limbs with sharpen sickles and broad-headed axes. A couple of the Wolfmen infiltrated the line, bringing down several of the bowmen. The onslaught did not abate. The Wolves continued to form new lines and charge forward. The soldiers and guards continued to rotate. Those receiving wounds fell back. Once patched up they returned to the battle.

CHAPTER 27

hat is going on?" asked Thangor as the noise of the battle drew his attention. "Guard, guard!" he called out. No one answered. Thangor released Talia and started toward the door. A rapping at the window stopped his progress and he moved to investigate. Thangor opened the window and came face to face with his own likeness. It was him; but not him. It looked like him, but it couldn't be him. He leaned closer.

Cybela smiled and with a gesture as quick as lightening lashed out with the blade. Thangor screamed and fell to the floor clutching his throat. Blood gushed from the gash across his throat. Blood seeped through his fingers as he gurgled his last breaths.

"Thangor!" Talia cried out, running and kneeling down beside him. A body leapt in through the window. Thangor stood looking down at her. But, he was also on the floor bleeding. She looked from the standing Thangor to the prone Thangor, her mind in confusion and disbelief.

Before she could make sense of what was going on, the shape shimmered like a mirage and changed shape. Talia was now looking up at herself, as if a mirror had been placed in front of her. She rose to face herself. Her hand moved to cover the scream growing in her throat. She reached out hesitantly to touch the specter standing before her. The image moved like a gust of wind and slammed into her.

Talia felt like she was being pressed to the wall. Her body convulsed and jerked, fighting for air as if she was under water. There seemed to be no ground beneath her feet, and nothing to grab or hold on to. She could not cry out or move her limbs. Fear and confusion raced through her mind as fast as the blood raced through her veins. A voice called out from the darkness laughing. *You are mine now.* Talia screamed and fell back on the bed. Everything went silent and black.

Cybela struggled to adjust, squirming and twisting like a snake shedding old skin. Slowly she gained control, flexing her new hands and stretching her new arms, savoring the feel of the young limbs. Closing her eyes, she focused inwardly. The new heart still pounded violently. Cybela gasped for air. Slowing her breathing, she sat erect. A rush of energy she had never felt before flooded through her. She stiffened at the intensity of it. Cybela let the feeling wash over her until she felt some control.

You're a powerful one, aren't you? I have never felt such...Ahh...such magnificent power. I see why everyone wants you. It is a good thing Phalon had me strike now. If you were a few years older I never would have been able to capture you. She laughed. *But now, I have.*

Cybela stood at the bedpost and steadied herself. Looking into the floor length mirror across the room, she ran her hands over her new face. Moving closer, Cybela stroked her new auburn hair and smiled at the new image before her. Gone were the fiery green eyes of Talia replaced by the hungry yellow eyes of a Wolf. Brushing her hands down the length of her dress, she gave her new look a passing shrug.

Cybela walked through the puddle of Thangor's blood, never giving his corpse a second look. She opened the door. The sounds of the battle echoed through the halls. Cybela sauntered toward the sounds leaving a trail of bloody footprints behind.

The power inside her pulsated and surged through her veins. She felt strong and invincible. "Never have I felt so alive. You have given me a great gift."

*C*yron grabbed his head, stumbled and fell against a tree. Regaining his balance, he looked around as if he were looking for someone.

"Are you all right Cyron? What's wrong?" asked Hanar.

Talia, Talia, where are you? Answer me, Talia. Fear overtook him. His eyes were bouncing around as his heart beat rapidly like that of a hummingbird.

"Talia. She's gone. I can't feel her anymore." His voice was high and strained.

"What are you saying?" asked Tyrel.

"She's gone." Panic was creeping into his voice. "It's as if she disappeared. She's not there anymore."

"Are you saying that she's dead?"

"No, he swallowed. "I don't think so. I don't know." The thought scared him.

"First, she was sad, then she was frightened, and then nothing. I just can't feel her anymore. It just stopped. Like she disappeared. Like she's..."

The possibilities of his words stuck him. His heart went cold as he finished his thought, "died".

"She's not dead!" Cried Hanar. "She's not dead!" He grabbed Cyron. "Say she's not dead!" His eyes were clouding.

"Please."

"She's too important to them. Of course, she isn't dead." Tyrel added. "It's just..."

"Just what?" demanded Cyron.

"I don't know. I don't understand magic," Tyrel said. "Let's just get to the manor and see for ourselves. Talia could have come up with something to confound them. She's brave and smart. She may be looking for us right now." His words were not convincing.

"Yes, yes. That's a good idea. We can't be sure of anything from out here." Hanar said anxiously. "Let's go."

"He's right. We'll go to the manor. You'll see, she'll be there." Tyrel half smiled and placed a hand on his friend's shoulder. "Come on Cyron don't give out on us now. We need you. Talia needs you."

Cyron looked into Tyrel's eyes searching for some sign of reassurance. Trying to hide his own doubt and fear.

"Alright. Let's go find her." The trio proceeded down the path toward the house. *We're coming.* He thought. But, received no answer.

Cybela descended the stairs like a queen making a grand entrance. Magic rushed through her veins quick as white water rapids. Flicking her fingers, she shot small bursts of magic into the air that popped and fizzled away. Giddy with the heat of such newfound power, she giggled like a child at play.

Standing expressionless at the base of the staircase, she surveyed the hastily arranged hospital the main room had become. The area was crowded with the bodies of wounded and dying fighters. A frantic rush of people moved from one side of the great room to the other. Female members of the household dashed about carrying bowls of water and wads of bandages. Their faces were strained with worry and urgency, and their eyes were full of worry and fright.

Others labored desperately to reassemble torn flesh, halting the flow of bloody wounds and stitching together ragged gashes. Others crashed about gathering weapons and assembling barricades.

Wails of pains were mixed with the shouts and curses from the ongoing battle. Angry voices shouted. "Bring more arrows! Don't let them break the line! Kill the savage beast! Repair that blockade." Others cried from their pains and fears.

Cybela walked to the front door. Without fear or concern, she moved through the line of pensive bowmen and into the battle. Striding forward as if she were out for an afternoon constitutional. She sidestepped dueling combatants and stepped over scattered bodies.

"Cybela?" called Phalon when he spotted her strolling his way. She nodded and smiled. He leaned back and crowed like a proud rooster welcoming in his first sunrise.

"C-y-b-e-l-a, Owoo, Owoo." The pack members, aware of the sign, began backing away from the battle, stepping over the mounds that were their fallen brethren. Clearing the path, they welcomed the young Sorceress into the fold. Happy yelps and snarls rang out. Cybela continued forward toward the center of the Wolf pack, her yellow eyes bright as suns.

Cannullus, strategizing with Lord Jannus, spotted Talia as the crowd began to clear away.

"Talia, what is she doing there?" he asked no one in particular. "Get back here before you're killed by those beasts!" he shouted. She turned to him and smiled.

Cannullus, confused by her reaction, grabbed the arm of the captain of the guard. "Her senses must be rattled. Send some men out there to get her back. Now!"

"Yes sir," answer the captain, pointing to a half a dozen soldiers. He ordered them out to retrieve her.

"Archers, prepare to fire. You will need to cover their return," he instructed the others. "Aim wisely. Don't hit the girl."

The soldiers advanced on Talia. "Stay there, young miss. We are here to help. We're coming to get you."

Cybela faced the oncoming guards. She looked at Cannullus, yellow eyes beaming with energy. Her smirk caused an uneasy feeling to creep over him. She extended her hands as if asking for help. Cybela felt the energy gather around here. It ran up her arms and seemed to spark from her fingertips. It crackled all around her. Every part of her vibrated, bathing her in a rush of power that made her lick her lips with delight. The feeling was delicious.

"I won't be needing your assistance," she told them. Letting loose a burst of energy, she launched the soldiers backward into the air. Cybela threw back her head and laughed with a joyous madness. "I'm going to like being you, little girl."

Phalon joined in baying with delight, clapping his hands and stamping the ground as if he were putting out a fire. Cannullus gasped, his eyes wide with the shock and unable to process the scene.

"Bring a horse!" shouted Phalon, as Cybela joined them. "You did it. You did it. We will be invincible." Cybela started to mount the horse.

She swayed and nearly slipped from the stirrups. Phalon moved in to aid her. Gripping the reins, she settled into the saddle.

Cybela raised her hand to her forehead. She felt the awakening of the young Sorceress inside her. Concentrating on the soldiers and not on controlling Talia had allowed the young woman to regain some small control and attempt to break free. Cybela acted to halt her efforts. *There is no use in fighting, Talia. I control things now. Your power is mine. You will never be free.*

Phalon asked, "Is everything all right?"

'It is very taxing what I have done. She fights me even now, trying to regain control. But she cannot. I will win. I just need to rest. All will be well." Cybela spurred the horse into a gallop. Phalon ran by her side. The pack followed, yelping and howling in victory, leaving their adversaries in total dismay and confusion.

Talia, what are you doing? Cannullus wondered. *How has Phalon gained control of you?* Anger rose in him. He shouted. "We must pursue them. We cannot let them get away with the girl. She is too important."

'But sir," the captain of the guards said. "...she went willingly. She attacked us."

'They have hexed her. Talia would never do that. Thangor will..." Cannullus stopped and looked around him. "Thangor. Where is the prince? Find the prince."

Three pairs of disbelieving eyes stared from a thicket at the edge of the woods. "She's not dead. But, what is she doing?" asked Tyrel. "Has she betrayed us and joined with the Wolves?"

"Talia would never betray us. And she would never join the Wolves." Hanar protested jumping to her defense.

"You saw her. She attacked the Humans and left with the Wolves. And they did not force her." Tyrel said.

"Something else is going on. Talia would never. Would she, Cyron?" Hanar asked looking for some reassurance.

Cyron stood transfixed. His eyes were wide open, but he only saw Talia. All his concentration was on her. Stretching out his thoughts like branches on a tree. *Talia, Talia it's me Cyron. Talk to me. Talia answer me please.*

The pack with Talia at the head paraded by the trio. Cyron grabbed his head and cried out. Fear, panic, and desperation cried out to him. *Cyron, help me!* If not for the loudness of the celebrating pack, they would have been heard and discovered.

"No, no" he shouted. Crying out in agony Cyron's front legs buckled and he doubled over.

"What's wrong Cyron?" A worried Hanar moved to aid him.

"Talia, she's...she's there... she's trapped. It was so loud. She was screaming for my help. I heard her shouting in my head. When they passed, our minds touched and...it was almost too much to take. She's locked away in a prison. A prison inside herself."

"In a prison?" spat out Tyrel. "She didn't look like she's in a prison to me. She just rode by like a queen."

"No...no. That's not Talia." Cyron pointed to the receding figure. "I mean it is Talia, but that's not her. They're controlling her."

"Phalon did yell out 'Cybela,'" Hanar eagerly added.

"Yes, yes that's it. She's their Shaman. Yes, it's Cybela. Somehow, she's in control of Talia. Just for that instant when they passed by I was with Talia. She's locked away and Cybela has control of her."

"That can't be." insisted Tyrel. "How could you do such a thing?"

"I don't know. Listen to me. The girl we saw was Talia, but she is not in control. That was not Talia, Tyrel. Believe what I am telling you."

"What are we going to do? What are we going to do?" Hanar chanted, dancing around and chewing on his fingers almost in tears.

Cyron searched the faces of his companions for answers. He turned to the escaping pack then to the manor and then again back to his friends. "This is magic. We need help. We need to talk to Ladena."

CHAPTER 28

*L*adena listened carefully as Cyron, Tyrel, and Hanar took turns relaying events.

"Phalon called her Cybela?" She asked.

'He yelled it," replied Hanar. The other two nodded their heads in agreement. "She rode away with them freely, not as a prisoner?"

'At the head of the pack as if she were leading them." Tyrel added. His companions agreed.

'What did you sense when she passed close to you, Cyron?'

He closed his eyes and hung his head. "I felt terrible pain and fear. I heard her calling to me for help. I tried to answer her back, but..." He cradled his brow. "...the feelings were so strong. I don't know if I made it through to her."

Ladena shook her head as she paced the room. Her walking stick striking a steady beat of thuds as she paced and thought. The eyes of the three young bucks followed her like kittens chasing yarn. Ladena paused resting back on her haunches. With the wrath of anger in her voice and the heat of rage in her eyes she slammed the point of her walking stick into the floor.

'Cybela used some old and wicked magic to meld with Talia. I would not have thought she had the skill to do it. If she is not rescued soon she will be lost to us for all time. Talia has the power to free herself, but she is young and not skilled enough to know it. Not wise enough to know how. Cybela, like me, is old and experienced. She has taken advantage of Talia's youth. Let this be a lesson to all of you." She wagged a wizened finger at them. "Wisdom is your most powerful weapon and your deadliest foe."

"What can we do? We can't beat magic with a sword or a bow and arrow." Asked Tyrel.

"Cyron?" Ladena's call drew his eyes up from the floor. "You know, don't you? You have felt it, have you not?" He pressed his lips together and nodded reluctantly.

"Know what, Cyron?" asked Hanar.

Ladena raised her brows and gave him a yes with the tilt of her head.

Cyron's eyes locked with his grandmother's. "I...I'm the only one who can help her. Talia cannot free herself alone. She needs my help." His eyes traced Ladena's face as if the words were written on it. "Just like Cybela, I have to join with her. Together as one we can defeat her."

Ladena bobbed her approval. "No one else can reach her. She is a prisoner, chained in her own body; in her own mind. Only you can reach her. Only you can help her."

"You're no Sorcerer," insisted Tyrel. "How are you going to do this?"

"He must. He is the only one." Ladena insisted.

"Cyron," Tyrel said, standing before him, his chest puffed up as if he was bracing for a blow. "I am sorry my friend. I don't see how this can be done. We have to accept it. She is lost to us." Tyrel stretched to his full height.

"There is no way we can allow this Cybela to live. The Wolfmen were a problem for us before. Now they have an even more powerful Shaman on their side, putting our clan in greater danger. I've got to warn my father. We could be under attack at any time. We have to strike them before they become even stronger." Tyrel lowed his head. "I'm truly sorry, Cyron." He bolted out of the door.

Cyron watched him leave before turning to Ladena. "He's right grandmother. I want to help Talia anyway I can. But, how can I? I have no magic. I'll never get close to her. If I did, what's to keep Cybela from killing me before I can do anything to help Talia? If I even knew how." Defeat dripped from his words like rainwater off a roof. He turned away and slumped against the wall.

"Cyron, my boy." Ladena laid a hand on his shoulder. "Talia's arriving has awakened the magic in you. You must know this to be true. You have felt it. You may have felt the magic inside of you all your life without knowing what it was. Shame on me for never taking notice of it." She pressed her hands to her breast.

"Do you think you could feel and communicate with Talia if there was not magic in you? She does not do it all on her own. You two are one, part of the same seed. What your special skills are, I do not know. They will come to your aid when you need them. That is the way of magic. You will have to reach deep within yourself and allow it to surface. Do not fear it. It is the only hope Talia has. She needs you. You must not fail her. If you don't help her, Cybela will keep her trapped until she withers and fades away."

"You are not alone, Cyron. I will help." A dewy-eyed Hanar softly whispered.

"Of course, you will," said Ladena reaching for his hand and smiling. Ladena moved to her table and began gathering jars and containers around her. "I will prepare some things for you. There is not much time. The longer Talia is a prisoner, the weaker she will become. You must get to her soon. She will need your strength."

"Why don't you use your magic against Cybela?" Hanar asked.

Ladena looked at the questioning face of the Satyr. "Do you wish me to harm Talia? To kill her? I could do battle with Cybela, but it would be Talia who would suffer the consequences. No, this must be done from within and Cyron is the only one who can go there."

"She's right, Hanar. My bond to Talia is special. No one else can do what I can do. It's me, or no one. This is a fight we must do together."

"You will be taking over command of the situation, sir?" asked Lucius.

Cannullus stared steely-eyed at the man. "The prince is dead. Who do think should take charge, captain?" Without waiting for a reply, he continued. "I have sent the prince's body to Mandoria with a letter explaining our circumstances. I am sure the king will whole-heartedly agree with my actions. Do you have a problem with that, Captain?" he emphasized his words by moving in uncomfortably close to the soldier.

"No, sir," Lucius snapped to attention. He cleared the nervousness from his throat. "Every able-bodied male over the age of thirteen has been recruited. They are armed and ready to avenge their prince."

"As they should be," said Cannullus, feeling confident. "We have to attack and destroy the pack before they have a chance to replenish their numbers. Make it understood captain that it was not Talia, but the Wolfmen's Shaman, Cybela, who killed Thangor. Talia is not to be harmed. She is one of us. She is a victim here. Our young Sorceress would never have harmed her future husband. And she never would have gone away with the Wolves if it wasn't for this enchantment she is under."

"It may prove difficult to ensure her safety, sir. The men saw her attack us. They saw her ride away with them."

"She was under the spell of that bitch Cybela," his voice rising as sharply as his anger. "That backstabbing Phalon planned this. I tried to warn Thangor of his treachery. I always said he shouldn't be trusted," Cannullus leaned in toward the captain. "Between us..."

He turned his back and walked across the room. "I told Thangor it was a mistake to deal with the Wolves, but he would not heed my warning. I told him that one day he would regret his alliance with them." He turned and faced the captain. "Phalon betrayed him to gain control of the girl. Make sure it is known that she must not be harmed. We need her."

"But sir, what if she uses her magic against us?"

Cannullus looked at the black cloth bag on the desk. "We have magic as well, Captain. After all I am a Wizard. Am I not?" There was threat and sarcasm in his voice. "Get the soldiers ready." He snapped. "We leave in an hour." The captain saluted and left the room.

'Cybela, you don't know it, but you have done me a service. Now that Thangor is out of the way, I will retrieve Talia, and there will be nothing to stand between me and my rightful destiny."

"Will you be able to find her?"

"I don't know, Hanar. I hope so. We should be at the Wolf- men's village soon. I will keep calling out to her. Maybe she will hear me. That is, if she is even at their village."

"Where else would she be?

'I don't know," snapped Cyron. "I don't know where she is. I don't know what I'm doing. I don't know what to do. I just don't know anything." He moved ahead of the Satyr and silently led the way.

The full moon bounced its light around the forest, illuminating every grass and leaf. The stilled hush of the faded light was like the peace before a battle. It was the kind of quiet that made you aware of the slightest change or movement around you. Silence so humble that you are forced to commune with your doubts, entertain your worries, and confront your every fear.

Cyron and Hanar quietly made their way, clutching to the hope they would not be too late. And somehow find a way to make things right. Cyron carried an overwhelming load of doubts. Hanar fumbled for ways to help.

"Maybe we should have tried to get Tyrel to come with us." Hanar suggested, breaking the uncomfortable silence.

"Tyrel feels he has repaid his debt. His thoughts are with the clan now. You heard him, Hanar. He has given up on Talia. I am afraid that if he was with us he would kill Talia instead of trying to release her from Cybela's hold."

"Yes, but..."

"But nothing. We are on our own," his voice becoming sharp and shrill. "You don't have to go on. Return to the village. I'll do this myself."

Hanar stopped and stamped his hooves. "Just like Talia can't free herself without your help, you can't do this without mine, whether you are willing to admit it or not. I am going, and that is all there is to it." Hanar jetted a determined chin at him. "Besides, she may be your sister, but I've known her longer than you have. She is my friend and I won't give up on her."

"What, you've known her for what...four or five days more than me. That gives you the right to tag along?"

"She is my friend and I care about her. I don't give up on my friends. Like my father used to say, 'Hanar, the only thing you ever give up on is giving up.'"

"What...I don't...If you..." The Centaur stumbled with his words till he saw the smile on the Satyrs' face. They shared a nervous laugh.

"I'm sorry, Hanar. I'm just..."

"I know," he replied shaking his head. "I am too, but somehow I know we'll be alright. We'll do this and save Talia."

They marched on side by side. *I hope you're right.* Cyron thought to himself.

CHAPTER 29

Cyron where are you? Can you hear me? I need you. Help me, please. The pleas fell silent, not even an echo of them could be heard. *I don't understand what's going on. How did I get here? What is this place? Cyron, I'm frightened. Why won't you answer me?*

The silence was wrapped up in endless darkness. Locked in a prison in her own mind, confused and frightened, Talia ran in circles railing against the blackness. Everywhere she turned there was endless nothing. She could feel no ceiling, no floors, or walls. It was as if she was hanging in midair, but it did not feel like floating. It was more like being submerged beneath a sea of black water, yet not drowning. The space around her pressed heavy against her like a thick woolen coat.

Only when the thoughts of Cybela taunted her was there any sound. The sound came from everywhere, pounding at her. Cybela's thoughts would travel through her as if they were her own; thoughts heavy and thick with hate and sarcasm. The shrill noises were like pins being stabbed into Talia's brain. Exploding into bouts of anger and fear, Talia clawed back like a feral cat. Exhausting herself, she collapsed into a limp ball of spent emotions.

Cybela stumbled against the wall of her cave, straining against the backlash. Talia's distress caused distress of its own. A film of sweat coated Cybela's brow. *Quiet down little girl. There will be no escape for you. Face the truth of it. You are defeated and will never be free. Your life is over. All that you were is mine.*

Who are you? Where am I? Why are you doing this? Talia struggled to understand what had happened to her.

Spent from the struggle, Talia's thoughts wandered, floating about aimlessly in and out of the moment, randomly creating wild images full of pain and heartache. Visions of the dying Thangor lying at her feet, his life's blood painting the floor like wax. The regret of her last words hung about her neck like a leaden chain.

"I hate you. I hate you." It was regret so real it ached like an open wound. "I'm sorry, Thangor. I didn't mean it." She cried out, ruing her words. The painful memory caused her to bubble up in agitation. Cybela would feel the effects and falter, grasping whatever was close, bracing herself against the barrage. Wrenching with the ache of trying to contain and control her captives erupting emotions, Cybela shuttered and cried out from the effort.

"Father," Talia whispered. The image sprang up and cut through her like a sharp wind. "I did not know. I didn't know." Another emotional quake rumbled through her mind. Sadness and sorrow mixed with anger and rage. Pangs of remorse and heartache vibrated through her world.

Cybela experienced the emotional storm and fought to press them back, clutching the side of a table on unsteady legs like a child taking its first steps.

"No, no. Stop it. Stop it." Cybela screamed, trying to withstand the torrent of emotions that rushed her like rapids against a dam. The emotions were so raw and ferocious, they were like claws ripping away her flesh. She thought these were attempts by her captive to free herself. It never occurred to her shriveled heart that this could be the result of sorrow.

The walls the Shaman had built could not hold back the rage that exploded when Talia thought of Cannullus. "He poisoned your father,"

Thangor's words were a hard slap to the face. *I did not trust in myself and accepted what was told to me. I ran away like a frightened child.* Hatred and malice roared through her.

You killed my father. You blamed me for it. You made me believe I had killed the person I loved most in the world. Cannullus I will...I will...

She raged in a fire of sensations. For a few seconds, the whole universe blazed into a blinding light. Talia was transformed into an inferno of white-hot energy. The air around her shimmered like ripples on a pool. The waves of heat shot out in all directions. The feelings were so intense, so full, for a moment she felt herself free. For an instant, she saw herself standing as herself in the Shaman's cave.

She was bright as the sun, her very presence melting away the mountain. Free and fluid like air. There, but not there. Real, but a ghost of herself. More than herself, but less than she could be. Talia's eyes glowed and her heart burned. Life burned from within her over powering everything it touched.

Cybela's eyes glowed and her heart burned. The waves were strong and overwhelming. They engulfed her. She was not the source. She was being consumed. Burned by the power of the source. She screamed out as the rush of energy washed over her.

Cybela wavered against the onslaught, flapping helplessly in the maelstrom like a ship tossing on the sea. Summing all that she was, Cybela called out to her gods for protection and rescue. They were not enough. The power won out. She blacked out from the strain.

Cybela awoke on the dirt floor crumpled and drained and covered in sweat and bile. Regaining her senses, her eyes danced around wildly searching for answers. Fear and doubt gripped her thoughts. Tensing at the possibility of another onslaught, the wisdom of trying to contain and control something so foreign, so powerful was beginning to seem foolish. To continue could mean her death.

You are more powerful than I thought possible. How can you dance so close to The Fire, so close to the source and not be consumed by it? How can one so young do this?

Cybela moved about her lair hunting for ideas and methods to aid her. The possibility of possessing so much power on one side excited her, but on the other the fear of it made her wary and cautious of the ability to command the source. Only Talia stood in her way. The source ran deeply in her. Envy and jealousy fueled her lust to have it. "Why should you be so blessed?" A scowl of disapproval marked her face. "If I cannot control this. I will free myself and end you."

CHAPTER 30

*C*annullus rode at the head of the assembled army. Buoyed by the report from scouts that the Wolfmen were celebrating and not massing for an attack, his confidence in their surprise assault was high. Phalon would never expect him to return so quickly or so boldly. They would attack, rescue Talia, and put at least one of the kingdom's enemies to an end. This would surely raise his prospects. The king would be most pleased that he had avenged his son's death and be forever in his debt. It would only be fitting for Cannullus to move into a position of more responsibility and authority.

'After all, I will have taken vengeance against the killers of his heir. All in the name of Mandoria, of course." Cannullus chuckled.

Things weren't going exactly as planned, but he was adaptable. The fact the scouts hadn't located Talia was his only concern. Despite his warnings, he knew that if anyone came upon her and had the opportunity to kill her they would. He had to make sure that didn't happen.

Where was she? Was Cybela still enchanting her? What more had they done to her? Would she be of any use to him if they had done something unspeakable to her?

The thoughts ran through him, vexing his mind. A man like

Cannullus did not like to be uncertain or without answers. "Questions can be bothersome. But, questions without answers can be deadly," he was fond of saying. In this case, it could prove deadly for Talia and at least inconvenient and unfortunate for him.

"With Thangor out of the way I can wed the wench. She'd be under my control, and she'd be my property. Her abilities would only bolster my position. The king already depends on me. After this, he will see me as his only worthy successor. If he does not, then he'll have to meet with an unfortunate illness."

The Soldiers and the Alserrians did not notice the two pairs of eyes that followed their progress. Hidden in the tall grasses, a Centaur and a Satyr studied their progress.

"This is the first good luck we've had." Cyron said. "We can use the distraction of their attack to find Talia. If we're careful, we can slip in and out without being noticed."

"That would be great. I was afraid we'd have to fight the whole pack by ourselves," Hanar admitted, swallowing a lump of nerves. "I don't really like the Humans that much, especially that Cannullus, but I'm glad they're here."

"I thought you liked everybody?" Cyron joked.

"I try to," he admitted. "I'd like them better if they were all like Talia. She's a good Human. I remember my father saying, 'Hanar it's alright to like everybody just remember it's not a requirement.'" He nodded an agreement.

"Can you tell where Talia is, Cyron? Do you feel anything?"

"I'm not sure. I think I sense something, but it comes and goes. It's more like lightning strikes in a heavy rain. I must sort out which is her and what is me. Remember I'm still new at this." He gave a strained smile hunching his shoulders.

"I'm not sure if what I feel is Talia or that squirrel over there." He pointed to gray squirrel tilting his head back and forth as it studied them.

"Are you scared?" Hanar asked hesitantly looking at him out of corner of his eyes.

"No...Of course not..." Cyron shot up into a tall stand, his chest jetting out. Releasing the bluster, he blew out a deep breath and leaned against a tree. "A little, I guess."

Cyron shook his head and looked down, confessing to a flower. "I don't know anything about magic. Ladena said it would come to me when I need it. What will come to me? And when it comes what am I supposed to do with it?" Cyron looked at Hanar.

"This is important. Talia's life is hanging on this. What if I make a mistake? Or can't control what happens?"

"I don't know, Cyron. Ladena knows what she's talking about. She wouldn't send us off with just this bag of bottles," Hanar held up the green bag full of vials. The glasses clinked as he jostled the bag around.

"Ladena believes in you. Talia believes in you. And I believe in you too. All you have to do is believe in yourself. We can do this. When the time comes you'll know what to do." He forced a smile. "We've got to."

"I hope you're right." Cyron still racked with doubt ran his fingers through his hair and stared unsure into the distance.

Phalon left the village and made his way to the abandoned silver mine Cybela called home. Entering the cave, he found her on the ground, curled in a ball and covered in sweat. She shivered as the pangs of emotion within her were subsiding.

"Cybela, what is wrong? How can I help you?"

Sitting up, squinting her eyes, and panting as if she had been running for her life, she said, "I will be alright. There is nothing you can do. This is a battle for control between the young Sorceress and me. Her will is stronger than I thought it would be. She has not yet accepted her fate. It may take some time, but I will prevail."

"I need you to hurry and win this battle. Soon we will have enough new members to attack the castle. I will need you to be at full power to aid in our victory."

"I do not know when I will have total control of her as..." Cybela grabbed her head in hands and howled. Phalon pulled away in shock.

Talia cried out. "Cyron, Cyron." Her emotions were a mixture of anger, fear and desperation. "Cyron, Cyron I know you are out there. Hear me. Help me."

Talia's cries caused Cybela to arch her back in pain. She clutched at Phalon. Raking her fingernails into his arm as she tried to cope with the growing intensity of the emotions.

"She seems to be getting stronger, not weaker. I don't understand it. It's as if she's gaining power. She should be wasting away," Cybela managed to mumble between grimaces.

"Cybela," Phalon helped her to her feet. He grabbed her shoulders and looking into the face of Talia searching for some sign of the Shaman. Only Cybela's yellow eyes told him he was not talking to Talia.

"I thought you had control. I saw you use her powers at the manor."

"At the time, she did not know what was going on. I was able to surprise and over power her. It seems the young Sorceress has regained her composure."

"Can you do it again? Can you get control of her and her power?" He shook her as if he were waking her from a sound sleep.

"Cybela, I need to know. Can you do this?" Worry etched on his face. "If you cannot control her, we will have to kill her. We can't let her go back to Cannullus or the Centaurs. They will use her against us."

"I can do this," Cybela lied. "It will just take more time."

"Time is something we do not have much of. Cannullus must be planning a return. He wants the girl. I know he will strike us. We must strike them first. You have until tomorrow. If you do not have control over her by then," Phalon furrowed his hairy brows. "We must kill her." He stormed out of the cave.

"No, you will not Phalon. I will not relinquish this power. I will master this. To kill her would be to kill me. I will not allow that." Cybela crumpled to the floor as another wave hit her.

Cyron, I'm here. Where are you?

Cyron stopped and looked around him. "It's her. It's Talia. I can hear her. I have been having feelings. I thought it was just my own doubts, but I know now. It's Talia. At first, I couldn't make out if it was her I was feeling. But, I was feeling her and didn't know it. I'm beginning to understand what I'm feeling."

"Where is she?"

"I'm not sure. She's close. I think." He shut his eyes and concentrated. *Talia, I'm here. We are coming.*

"She must be in the village." Hanar brightened. "Is she alright?"

"Wait. There's something between us. It's keeping me from getting too close." He angled his head sideways as if he was looking at something around a corner.

"Cybela," he straightened up with a scowl on his lips. "It's Cybela. She's been blocking me. No, wait. She...she doesn't know I'm there. She's not trying to keep me out. She's trying to keep Talia in. I don't think she knows I'm here." He shook his head. "I mean there."

"You've got to find out where she is, Cyron." Hanar scratched his head. "Then we've got to figure out how to get her out of Talia. I hope some of these things Ladena gave us will help." He looked in the bag. "Maybe Talia will know how to use them."

"I don't think they'll help us free Talia from Cybela. Ladena said they would explode." The cries of battle interrupted his thoughts. Cyron reared up on his back legs to get a better look.

"The Humans are attacking. We need to go now. We've got to find Talia before they do."

"Where is she?"

"I told you. I don't know."

"You're the only one of us talking in his head. You've got to try harder. We don't have time to search the whole village." Hanar started and stopped, not sure which way to go.

Cyron concentrated and called out with determination. *Talia, Talia, where are you? Help me. I don't know where you are.*

The shouts and screams were getting closer as more Wolves joined the battle. "Look out behind you!" A soldier shouted. "They're in the tree!" yelled out another.

"Damn them," cursed yet another. Howls and growling mixed with shouts and screams until the sounds seemed to be coming from every bush and tree.

"Set fire to the shacks!" someone ordered. "There are too many of them" yelled a young man armed with a farmers' sickle.

"I'm hurt," cried out a man with claw marks down his back.

"You killed my son!" screamed an angry man as he charged at a group of three Wolves.

"Sound the alarm!" howled one Wolfman.

"It's the Humans! Kill them!" growled another. Baying and howling echoed through the trees as Wolfmen rallied to join the battle.

The captain of the guards shouted out commands trying to maintain order in his makeshift army.

"Don't let them out flank you." He ordered to one group. "Finish him off. Don't just leave him to attack someone else," he barked at a startled youth standing over a wounded Wolfman.

"Maintain that line. Bring up the rear." The captain pointed at a group who had eased their advance.

Weapons swung through the air, slashing and ripping bodies apart. Claws and fangs ripped and tore away hunks of flesh. Bushes and trees were splattered with random body parts. Blood gathered in dirty pools covering the ground. The stringent scent of death lingered in the air. Rampaging men set everything afire. Soon almost every building was ablaze, threatening to set the surrounding forest on fire.

Phalon howled with fury. Cannullus had taken away the time he thought he had. Phalon dashed back and forth through the throngs of soldiers and villagers, slashing and clawing at any he encountered. Leaping from the limbs of trees, he pounced on one group and dashed off to attack another. Catapulting from atop a burning building, he collided with a stand of horses bringing the soldiers and their animals to the ground.

The Wolfmen, some with weapons and some without, ran out of burning shacks to join their brethren in defending their homes. The smell of blood excited their senses. The rush of war was emboldening everyone.

Cannullus, staying well off to the side and away from the battle, scanned the area looking for signs of magic; for anything that might lead him to Talia.

Surely Phalon would use Cybela in this fight. It would be a perfect time to test her new abilities.

Equipped with a potion to produce a sleeping gas, he sought to subdue and capture the young Sorceress.

Once I have her restrained, removing Cybela may be difficult, but I will have time. I can keep her drugged till I find a way. he thought. Cannullus narrowed his eyes.

Use her now, Phalon. She won't be yours very much longer.

Cyron! called out Talia sending Cybela into convulsions. *The cave. The mine. The cave.*

As Cyron got closer, Talia seem to get stronger. He renewed her spirit and she bolstered his confidence.

Cave, cave, repeated Cyron. *She's in a cave. The mine. The cave of the old silver mine.*

"Isn't the silver mine on the other side beyond the village?" Hanar asked. He looked around blinked and swallowed nervously.

"How do we get there? Do we have to fight our way through the village? Or do we go around the battle?"

Cyron surveyed the scene. He nodded his head and said, "Here's what we're going to do. You get on my back and we'll charge a path through the village."

"Through the village? That's...that's crazy! That's where the battle is."

Cyron smiled. "It's time to try out Ladena's exploding potions." Hanar reluctantly assented and climbed on Cyron's back.

"Are you ready?" Cyron asked the trembling Satyr, who responded with a hesitant "yes..." and Cyron bolted for the village. "We're coming Talia. Hang on tight, Hanar!"

CHAPTER 31

*G*alloping at full speed, Cyron leapt over fallen trees and bodies. "Down!" he yelled at Hanar as he skirted a barrage of arrows, ducking under the quills as if they were the branches of a tree. The frightened Satyr tugged at Cyron's hair holding it like a lifeline. His thighs hugged Cyron so tight that his knees ached from the strain.

Pivoting around a burning shack, Cyron impaled a Wolfman with a spear he snatched up that was lying next to a dead villager. Racing forward, a wall of heavily armed soldiers blocked his way.

"Time to try one of Ladena's concoctions." Hanar said retrieving one of the vials. He kissed it before he threw it as they got near the angry barrier.

Cyron stopped and they watched. The bottle somersaulted through the air end over end, and landed in front of the soldiers. They looked at the bottle lying at their feet, then at each other, and then back to Cyron and Hanar. Their puzzled faces were replaced by angry sneers as they stepped forward to confront them.

The bottle exploded into a bright ball of light and a bang louder than any they had ever heard cracked the air like a rock shattering glass. The explosive force sent the group of soldiers flying through the air to land stunned and dazed on their backsides. Cyron and Hanar stared at each other. They exchanged a laugh and gave each other a nod of approval. Energized, Cyron took off again. Racing through the opening created by the blast. "We're coming, Talia!"

Sword in hand, Cyron impaled a charging Wolfman and slashed the leg of a slow moving farmer wielding a sickle. He plowed down a crouching Wolfman who was posed to leap on a retreating soldier.

Hanar threw three more exploding bottles; one at a trio of Wolfmen trying to overrun them. The blast left them stunned and bloodied. Hanar threw another bottle at a group of archers taking aim from the shelter of a rocky overhang. The explosion brought the rocks down on them in a dusty heap.

The third bottle was thrown at a cluster of Wolfmen and Soldiers between two burning buildings whose scuffle obstructed their path. The blowup sent the group scrambling in different directions. Hanar laughed at the spectacle like a kid with a new toy.

Cyron displayed his skill with a bow, picking off half a dozen attackers and sending them flying backward, impaled by his arrows. He noticed for the first time how he didn't seem to need to aim. Arming the bow seemed to be enough. If he could picture the target in his mind the arrow would obey. *Was this magic? Have I been using magic all along and didn't know it? Was Ladena right?* he wondered.

Two pairs of anxious eyes took special notice of the loud distractions that echoed through the battlefield. One pair belonged to Phalon. He spotted the spirited Centaur and his eager hitchhiker dashing through the village. Seeing the escaped Centaur back in his mist infuriated him. He swiped through the throat of a quivering townsman and took off in pursuit of the duo, raining chaos on any that stood in his way.

Cannullus was the other pair of eyes, perched at a safe distance from the carnage, he registered the blast as well. Recognizing the presence of magic, he insisted on an escort for his protection so he could investigate. They galloped off cautiously, weaving their way through the destruction.

Cybela crouched in a crevice in the cave wall holding her head in agony. She felt her control waning. The presence of the young Sorceress was becoming larger and larger as she reclaimed territory. Cybela felt herself being pressed as if she were being forced into a too-small box. The eyes that had become a wild yellow when the She Wolf first possessed Talia were now one yellow and the other its original green. The young Sorceress was growing stronger and resisting Cybela's every effort. With each passing hour Talia was more viable and Cybela felt more like a phantom. She feared soon Talia would be strong enough to evict her from her body, or to destroy her.

Frantically, she searched for a way to escape what had turned into torture. *How can I free myself of this? What will become of me if I can't stop her from regaining control?* Each question, each doubt weakened her hold and allowed Talia to move one step closer to freedom.

Cybela could feel the young Sorceress' thoughts boring into her mind like worms moving through and apple core. With each push forward, Talia felt herself absorbing the shaman and growing stronger.

*C*yron raced past the last shack of the village and headed for the tree line. Once safely out of sight of the village, they stopped to catch their breath. Hanar hopped off Cyron's back and pocketed the last exploding bottle.

"That was wild!" Hanar said. "Ladena sure surprised me. Those exploding things really had a punch." He laughed. "Did you see the expressions on their faces when that vial exploded and sent them flying? I laughed so hard I almost fell off your back."

"My favorite was when that overhang crashed down on those soldiers. They thought they were safe in their hiding place. That really showed them!"

Cyron and Hanar enjoyed laughing at their escapade through the village, but Talia interrupted their celebration.

With his heart slowing down enough for him to pay attention to what else he was feeling, Cyron went rigid. Talia wasn't calling out to him, but her presence was so intense, so vibrant, that it reached out and touched him. He felt himself merging with her. He was there with her, seeing, feeling, and sharing everything. They fed off each other and revitalized each other at the same time. They were two separate beings, but one soul. The link between them went beyond the physical and the mental. They were one life, one being. The thread that linked them lived in the fire. It existed in the flames in the heart of the fire.

It was magical, comforting, and frightening all at the same time. Cyron was transfixed. He stood before Talia. They stared at each other and shared a knowing smile. A moment of clarity passed between them. It all seemed so obvious, so clear, and so right. What she could channel, he could absorb. What he could absorb she could channel. He was a vessel and she was a spout. She was the end to his beginning. They were a closed circle. Ladena's words came back to him.

"What your special skills are, I do not know. They will come to your aid when you need them." Cyron's mind opened up like the lid on a box.

"Cyron, are you alright?" The nudge and the words of the Satyr brought him out of his dream state.

"I'm fine," he said calmly. "I understand." He smiled looking out into the distance as if he never had eyes before.

"Understand what? Did you get hit in the head by a tree branch or something?"

"No, my friend." he laughed. "Let's go get my sister." Hanar eagerly agreed. They made their way toward the mine entrance, avoiding open spaces by staying close to the trees, and being careful not to draw any attention to themselves. Although the battle inside the village still raged on, there still could be stragglers lurking in the woods.

Cannullus and his escort wove their way through the village, skirting the many pockets of fighting. Following the trail of blast holes and bodies they made a path toward the mine.

Cybela is becoming very adept with Talia's powers. Powers I should be controlling, he thought as he surveyed the damage.

"Remember," he shouted to the guards through clenched teeth.

"She is not to be harmed. She's under the Shaman's magic. I will deal with her."

Phalon fought his way through the crowd of combatants, encountering heavy resistance as groups of Soldiers recognized him and called for his head. He fought and ran and had to double back again and again. Eluding the Soldiers and Townsmen was infuriating and exhausting him. Leaping into trees and off of burning buildings, he cut a zigzag route through the village.

They're trying to rescue the young Sorceress, he thought. *I should have killed her when I had the chance.*

The burning shacks spread fire to the surrounding trees, illuminating the area. Screams, shouts, howls, and crashes could be heard echoing against the roar of the fire. The wind whipped up the flames and smoke, creating dense clouds that made it difficult to see the clusters of hiding Soldiers and Wolfmen laying in ambush. Cyron and Hanar spotted Cannullus and his guards as they rode out from the chaos at the edge of the village.

The two moved back behind a boulder in just enough time not to be seen. A Wolfman, bloodied and frothing at the mouth, emerged from behind a burning shack. He howled and hurled a large rock that struck the hindquarters of Cannullus' horse. Staring down the Wizard, he charged. The oldest of the guards, a man with a nasty scar across his cheek and an attitude to match, broke ranks, circled around the deranged creature, and impaled him with his sword. He rejoined Cannullus and the other guard with a look of amused satisfaction on his face. His actions were rewarded with a look of bored distain. Cyron and Hanar allowed the trio to gallop past.

"I hate that Wizard," whispered Cyron. "We're going to have to take care of his guards before we deal with him. Quietly though, we don't want to attract any attention."

"All right," answered Hanar timidly. "What do you want me to do?"

Cyron saw the apprehension in his face. "Don't worry, Hanar. You won't have to kill anyone. The Satyr visibly exhaled. "I just may need you to distract them while I get in place."

Hanar nodded eagerly. "I can do that. No problem."

"One of you remain here and guard the entrance. The other come with me," Cannullus ordered, dismounting and heading for the cave entrance. The older guard signed to the younger to take a position at the opening. Cannullus and his companion proceeded into the opening.

'Alright, Hanar. What I want you to do is run out like you're headed for the cave. When he sees you turn and start back toward the village. I'll do the rest."

Hanar took a couple of deep breaths. "I'm ready. Tell me when you want me to go."

Cyron patted him on the back. "Go, go now."

Hanar raced out like a jackrabbit being chased by a fox. When he saw the guard had noticed him he stopped, looked around like he didn't know where to go. The guard drew his sword and started toward him. Hanar turned and started for the village. The guard broke out into a run. As he passed the boulder they were using for cover, Cyron leapt out and smashed him on the head with the hilt of his sword. The guard fell like a rock. Hanar ran back to him and together they dragged his body behind the boulder.

"That was good work. The next one may not be so easy."

"We're a good team. We'll handle it." Hanar beamed.

"I think you're right." Cyron agreed. His expression got serious. "I've been trying to connect with Talia. She senses me and knows we're close. But all of her concentration is on defeating Cybela."

"We need to get in there and help."

"Going by what Talia told me, we've got to be careful of Cannullus. He is sneaky and deadly."

"Like a snake..." Cyron grunted.

CHAPTER 32

*C*yron and Hanar disappeared into the darkness of the cave's entrance. The sounds of the battle became muffled and were lost to the blackness as if they had closed a door. Cyron led the way, with Hanar creeping close behind. Their eyes slowly became accustomed to the lack of light. As they felt their way along the wall, the passage opened into a large chamber. The diffused light of dozens of oil lanterns and candles illuminated the room. In the distance, voices could be heard. Cyron and Hanar peeked around the corner.

The room was outfitted with several stone tables and a fire pit against a far wall. Bowls and vials holding a lively array of substances sat on the tables. Animal parts and plants swam in a collection of containers. The smell of sulphur, mint, and burning coals hung in the air, stinging their noses. The cave floor was covered in a thick mist that clung to their legs like wet clothes. Cybela crouched on a chair like a cat ready to pounce on a mouse. Her expression was wild and sinister. Cannullus and the guard stood across the room from her. The guard presented his sword forward ready to defend. The Wizard looked around nervously, fumbling in his pocket to secure his vial.

"I know, Cannullus, which means that she knows as well," Cybela croaked.

'You know nothing, Witch. I will give you one chance to release Talia or I will."

"Will what? Kill us both?" She laughed. Her voice was shrill and biting. "You do not have the power or the skills to force me out. And as I said, she knows that you poisoned her father. Your little plan to kill him and blame her has been revealed. She knows how you used his injuries to make it look like she killed him. If I were to release her now, are you sure she would not kill you?" Cybela wagged her finger as she continued, "Tsk, tsk bad Wizard."

"Cannullus killed my father," Cyron whispered. "That's the secret Talia was hiding. The thing she was shielding me from finding out." He pressed his hands into fist. "I'll kill him."

"I'm so sorry, Cyron." Hanar laid a hand on his shoulder. "And poor Talia carrying that guilt all this time and she hadn't done anything."

Cyron didn't answer. He trembled with rage.

Talia, he reached out a plea in his thoughts. *I'm here, sister. I'm with you.*

Talia felt the incoming energy of Cyron's presence. Cybela reacted by rising to her feet. She cupped her head and screamed. Cannullus and the guard stepped back frightened by the outburst. Talia shouted, beating the void around her. "You will not take my life. I will rule my own destiny."

Cybela felt herself being sucked inward. She rocked in the chair and tumbled to the ground. Talia felt herself emerge back into the world like a chick breaking out of an eggshell. On her hands and knees, she looked up at Cannullus. Her eyes, both green now, radiated hate and loathing. Cybela struggled to resurface. Talia slammed her hand on the ground and a door closed in her mind, sealing Cybela like a bug in a jar. Cybela screamed and shouted as the space around her closed in on her like a coffin.

Talia stood straight and erect, her shoulders squared and her face a mask of granite. "You killed my father." Her voice was both sad and threatening. "You poisoned him and blamed me." A wave of pure hatred radiated from her. Her emotions reached out and engulfed the Wizard.

Cannullus convulsed and twitched dropping his vial to the floor. The glass broke and the gases faded with a hiss into the mist. He began rising from the ground as if an invisible hand had sieged him. Suspended in midair, he kicked and gasped for air. Talia's eyes bore into him. They were green pools of hate.

Cyron was pulled in by her emotions. Swept up in the gathering storm his green eyes began to glow. He faced the Wizard. Joined in a tempest of anger, their fury assaulted him from two sides. The room throbbed like the heart of a star. Waves of heat pulsated in the air causing Hanar and the soldier to raise their arms to shield their faces.

The guard stepped toward Talia, his sword raised to strike her. Before his third step, one of Cyron's arrow protruded from his chest. He died before he hit the ground. Hanar stepped back his mouth agape with shock. Cyron had not drawn an arrow or aimed his bow. He had not laid his hands on it. Just his desire to do it had sent the arrow flying. Cyron seemed unaware of what he had done.

Cannullus kicked in the air like a butterfly caught in a web. His legs and arms flapped about. His guttural screams fell on uncaring ears. The long brown robe he wore began to smoke. He pulled and yanked at the fabric as it became hot to the touch and searing his fingers in a feeble attempt to undress.

"You killed my father," Talia and Cyron mumbled in unison. A wind swirled around them. Their hair streamed about their heads as the gust grew. Their eyes glowed with an emerald fire. Linked as one mind, they shared a single thought, one desire: vengeance.

"No, no! It was Thangor's idea! I only did as I was ordered!" Cannullus screamed, pleading for mercy. The heat in the room increased. Steam and smoke rose from the Wizard. He shouted and hollered as he twisted in pain.

A dark shadow charged into the room. Phalon crashed into Cyron and Hanar. With a well-placed elbow, he clubbed the Centaur in the head. "You have caused me enough trouble, boy." Cyron dropped to the dirt floor. The connection broken, Talia faltered and collapsed to her knees. Cannullus, released from the dual assault fell to the ground. He cried and whimpered with a mixture of pain and relief, his robe cloudy with smoke and steaming red blotches covering his body.

Cybela, feeling her restraints eased, attempted to reassert herself. She reached out and was repulsed by the wall of flames burning in Talia's mind. She shrieked with frustration. Talia's mind flared. The fire pushed the She Wolf back deeper into the recess of Talia's mind. Caught in a whirlpool of raw emotions, Cybela sank further into a dark abyss.

Hanar rose from the floor stunned and confused. Blocked by the raging Wolfman, he stood paralyzed with fear. Stepping back, he melted into a shallow crevice in the wall.

Phalon, with sharp jerking movements, scanned the room, his chest heaving with a desire to attack, his muscles pulsating from the need to strike out.

"Cybela?" he growled running and stooping before Talia. She slowly lifted her head to meet him eye to eye. He reared back when the green eyes of the young Sorceress flared at him.

Feeling in control, Talia stood tall. "Cybela is no more." Her voice was sure and defiant. The air around her shimmered. Balancing on the balls of his feet, Phalon snarled and raised his arms to strike her down. Talia held up her clenched fists. Like a coiled snake they sprang open sending a blast of energy at Phalon that sent him across the room somersaulting over one table and crashing into another. The stone table cracked in two and rested like a tombstone over him.

Hanar ran to Cyron. "Cyron, Cyron are you alright?" The Centaur slowly reacted, rubbing the back of his head. He rose on shaky legs and fell back against the wall.

Cannullus, whimpering in pain, crept on his hands and knees toward the cavern opening. His face and body were covered in charred skin and blisters. His robe was smoking like a tobacco pipe. Wrenching with the effort, he clawed his way forward.

Talia focused once again on Cannullus. With measured steps, she moved toward him, circling him as if she were a moon orbiting a planet. Her eyes closed to slits like knives. The air around her popped and crackled with energy.

Phalon roused and slithered up from the floor. Climbing onto one of the remaining tables like a vine creeping up a trellis, he perched on all fours. Blood and dirt matted his wiry hair. He snared like a mad dog. Fangs wet with saliva appeared behind his trembling lips. He sprang for her.

"Talia, look out!" Hanar shouted, diving and tackling her to the ground and out of the Wolfman's reach. Phalon's claws missed her, but dug into Hanar's back, tearing a bloody trench. Talia and Hanar fell face down onto the floor. Hanar screamed in pain.

Arrows began flying around the room. Phalon with the speed of a bolt of lightning jumped and dove about, dodging arrows that flew with a will of their own. Seeking cover wherever he could find it, he managed to avoid a killing shot. Several arrows scraped him leaving glancing wounds. Cyron galloped to their side and helped Talia lift the wounded Satyr.

"Phalon, help me." Cannullus pleaded, reaching out with begging hands. "Help me please."

Phalon looked down and spit on him. "You are no concern of mine, Wizard. Crawl back to your castle and die." He ran at him and slashed him across the face. Cannullus cried out in agony. The Wolf-man's claws left deep gashes that gushed blood down his blistered face. The Wizard rolled against the wall cupping his face. Phalon circled the trio; a look of disgust and anger on his face. "Where is my Cybela? What have you done to her?"

"She is no more. She chose her fate and now she has it." Talia replied, a bit of pride and satisfaction in her voice.

"Grr. You will pay for this. I will not be denied. I will have my revenge." Phalon moved like the wind toward the entrance. He over-turned two barrels of black viscous oil. The oil splattered and spread about covering most the floor. Cradling a lantern, he heaved it into the center of the spill. The floor erupted in a wall of smoky flames. Everyone covered their eyes from the ignition. The blaze quickly grew, forcing them back deeper into the cave. Thick black smoke billowed up, causing everyone to collapse into fits of coughing and heaving. Nothing could be seen but flames and smoke.

Cannullus shrieked out in horror as the oil soaked his robe and burst in flame. The Wizard gasped and screamed as he rolled around in the oil and fire. The flames engulfed him licking the skin from his body. His screams of anguish were lost in the roar of the fire. He screamed until there was no more of him left.

'Not so high and mighty now, are you, Cannullus?" Phalon howled with laughter. "Die, all of you!" he shouted as he moved out of the passage.

"How are we going to get out of here?" Hanar coughed, wincing with pain. "Talia, blow a hole in the wall."

"No!" Yelled Cyron. "That might bring the mountain down on us."

"The only way out," Talia said. "…is straight ahead through the fire."

"The fire?" Hanar responded.

"Yes. The fire." Talia answered. "Cyron, I will need your help."

"Talia," Cyron asked. "Can you do this?"

"Just as Cybela had control of me and knew everything I did, now that I have control of her, I have gained her knowledge." Talia stared into the flames. She bit her lip. "I can do this."

"Alright," he nodded. "What do you want me to do?"

"Just concentrate with me. We will build a tunnel through the flames." she said. Hanar groaned.

"Help me get Hanar on my back." The wounded Satyr climbed on his back. He hugged him around the neck and closed his eyes. Cyron swallowed and took Talia's hand. Their minds met in midair like clouds joining to form a storm.

"Think of nothing but a tunnel. Imagine it like a passage through the forest."

The cavern seemed to shift and alter its shape. Spirals of flames arched over their heads like the canopy of a tree. Sheets of flames encircled them. They did not burn or sear. The flames gathered around them like a wall. Smoke swirled around creating a barrier between them and the heat.

"See it," whispered Talia.

"Yes," Cyron mumbled his eyes full of fascination and dread. With every surge of the flames he gripped her hand tighter. They stepped forward. The flames surrounding them became denser and brighter as they moved ahead. With every step, the tunnel forged forward. Cyron felt Talia's thoughts strengthen and encourage him. Talia felt his support and trust. Matching step for step, their confidence in their path and each other increased.

Hanar held on to Cyron's neck like a drowning man clinging to a log. Every time he opened his eyes, he'd slam them shut and grip a little tighter. His words were lost to his frantic panting.

The flames pushed onward, cutting a path through the burning oil and smoldering mist of the cave. Talia grimaced when they passed the desiccated remains of Cannullus. Her hatred momentarily replaced by disgust.

Father has been avenged came the thought from Cyron. She squeezed his hand and stepped ahead.

Stepping out of the cavern and in the passageway, the trio stopped. The flames slowly faded away as they eased themselves against the wall.

"You can open your eyes now, Hanar. We've made it. We're through the fire." Cyron said, jostling the Satyr to the ground.

"You two are scary!" Hanar exclaimed, arching his back from the pain of his wounds. "I was sure we were going to roast alive in there."

"Very funny, Hanar," Talia said. "Lay still for a minute and let me see if I can do something about those cuts."

"You're not going to do magic on me, are you?" he protested, as he lay on his side.

"Does everything scare you?" Cyron asked.

"No, it's just that..."

"Be still." Talia insisted. "Ladena taught me how to use my gifts to help cure as well as destroy."

"Alright," he relented. "Just be careful. I don't want to end up like Cannullus."

The mention of the Wizards name made Talia pause. Thoughts of her father flooded her mind.

Father, if I had only known.

"Don't blame yourself anymore, Talia. You didn't kill Talleon. Your magic is not to blame. I'm sure he knew how much you loved him," Cyron laid his hand on her shoulder. "Cannullus is to blame. His greed and envy killed Father. Cannullus got what he deserved."

He knelt down beside her. "It will be all right now. Father would be glad that you are here with Ladena and me."

"And me, too." added Hanar.

"Yes, with you too, Hanar." Cyron laughed.

"Now be still." Talia laid her hands on the wound across his back. She felt the heat and the pain build. She jerked back her hands.

"What's wrong?" asked Cyron.

Talia shook her head. "It's just that at first you feel the pain. Never mind. Let me start again." She laid her hands on the deep scratches. The warmth flowed down her arms and filled her hands, spreading out onto Hanar's scarred back. She bit her lips as the pain flowed back into her. Slowly it eased, becoming fainter and fainter.

"That feels funny. But, it doesn't hurt anymore." Hanar said.

"I'm not as good as Ladena is at this, but that should keep you until we get back to her."

"Talia," Cyron asked. "What was that I felt in there? It felt so strange. It was unlike anything I've ever felt before."

She smiled. "That was The Fire, the magic in you."

"But I'm no Sorcerer. I don't do magic."

"There is magic in you, Cyron. We both have it. I couldn't have done that without you."

Cyron looked both confused and worried. "But..."

"Don't worry about it. There will be time for you to understand it."

Cyron moved down the passage, his brows heavy with doubt and concern. He just stood there, unable to get his mind around the magic. A familiar sound brought him out of his contemplation.

"Do you hear that?"

"Hear what?" asked Talia.

"Don't tell us," Hanar said, exasperation in his voice. "You're hearing other voices in your head now."

Cyron gave him a look that caused him to look away in embarrassment. "No," he said. "That sound. It sounds like a horn, a battle horn. A Centaur battle horn." He ran to the cave entrance.

Talia helped Hanar to his feet and they followed. Cyron stopped at the opening. The dawn was beginning to peer over the horizon. The light of day revealed the stark realities of war. Laid sprawled amidst the burned-out buildings and charred forest were the twisted bodies of Wolfmen and Humans alike, spread out like broken toys covering the ground. Most of the village and the surrounding forest was now a memory drenched in ash. All that remained standing were blackened sticks that were once majestic trees, and jagged pieces of lumber that were once parts of walls. Red tinted mud puddles dotted the area. A putrid stench hung in the air.

The sounds of battle echoed in the distance; shouts and screams and clashing metals. A horn blast sounded across the desolate landscape, and then everything fell silent.

With a look of surprise and confusion on his face, Cyron cantered in place like a stallion eager for a race.

"We've got to get down there. The Centaurs have joined the battle."

"The Centaurs? But how?" Hanar asked.

"Tyrel must have convinced Marreanus to join in and come to our aid."

"Look around you. The Wolfmen are dead," said Talia. "They must be battling with the Humans."

"All the Wolfmen can't be dead. Phalon is still out there," closing his eyes to angry slits.

Talia swayed and raised her hand to her forehead.

"Are you alright?" Cyron asked.

"It's Cybela. Every now and then I feel her."

"Where is she?" Hanar asked, looking around ready to pounce.

"You don't understand. She's trapped inside me. I have to fight to keep her there. It takes a lot of energy to keep her locked away."

"She's still in your head? Really?" he asked, disbelieving. "Well, I guess that's no stranger than her being in your head."

"Yes, I suppose not. I think I'll need Ladena's help to rid myself of her."

Hanar gave her a skeptical glance as they headed off toward the battleground.

CHAPTER 33

*T*he area looked like an excavation at a cemetery. Severed limbs and mangled bodies lay in piles like driftwood. Footprint puddles of crimson water made a path through the village. A sickening smell of death and decay hung in the air. The remnants of spent arrows, splintered spears, broken axes, and other discarded weapons poked out of the ground. It was a bizarre crop growing on a field of death. Blood dripped from them like rain falling off a roof. Wisps of smoke trickled up from smoldering bits of burnt and charred trees and buildings. The eerie silence was broken by an occasional gasp of someone exhaling their dying breath.

Marching a zig-zagging path, the group made their way through the grizzly maze, their eyes riveted to the carnage that laid around them. No one could find the words to express their shock.

Cyron lead the way, Hanar followed, with Talia tagging behind. Dead eyes watched as they walked around the carnage. A quiet melancholy settled over the trio. They tiptoed as if they were trying not to wake the dead. While passing an extremely smoky pile of timbers, a figure darted out and grabbed Talia.

Phalon snarled and sneered, saliva dripping from his fangs. Holding Talia in a one-armed embrace he held his other claw at her neck. "Attack and I will rip out her throat." Phalon whispered to Talia. "Try your magic and I will kill you before the spell is cast."

Cyron and Hanar froze, unsure how to act. Phalon smiled and nuzzled her hair. "You have cost me everything, Witch." He whispered in her ear. "All my people. All my plans." He paused. "And Cybela. My lovely Cybela."

Talia's eyes darted about looking for an escape. She struggled against Phalon's grip, but the Wolfman was too strong.

"What do you want, Phalon?" Cyron asked.

"What do I want? What do I want?" he growled, his voice growing in pitch and volume. He laughed. His eyes glazed over as if a fog had descended from his brain.

"What I want you cannot give me boy. There is nothing left but revenge. I will make sure that you...that all of you pay for what you have done."

Talia what can I do? he thought. Cyron's eyes searched her face for an answer.

Nothing. Stay back I will deal with this. she replied. Talia eased her mind and spoke. "Cybela is not gone."

Phalon gripped her tighter causing her to grunt. "Where is she? Let her come back to me. Then maybe I will let you live."

"She is with me." Her voice was calm and enigmatic. "She is a part of me. If you kill me, you kill Cybela too."

Phalon bristled at the revelation. "Release her or I will kill you both."

Cyron, I will need your help. I need you to be with me. Cyron nodded. Hanar's head bounced back and forth from Talia to Cyron looking for a sign of what was going on.

"Now, Witch!" Phalon demanded.

Talia began gathering the energy around her, her stare a defiant wall. She felt the support and presence of Cyron bolster her waning strength. The air began to stir. There was a tremor in the ground. The temperature began to rise.

Phalon sensed something was going on and gripped her tighter.

His claws bit into her side. Talia winched at the pricks into her skin. His eyes danced about as he felt the heat building.

"What...What's going on?" He stepped back almost falling over a smoldering log. His grip loosened.

"Phalon," the raspy voice of Cybela reached out. "Help me, Phalon." He spun Talia around and stared into her face. "Cybela, are you still in there? Come back to me." Franticly, he searched Talia's face hunting for a sign of Cybela.

Talia jerked her arms free. Reaching deep within herself, she forced Cybela to come forth, spitting her out like a discarded pumpkin seed. The formless essence of Cybela, seeking a vessel, spilled into Phalon. He howled, grunted and jerked about uncontrollably. The Wolfman seemed to swell then deflate. One moment he was Phalon and the next he was Cybela, then Phalon again. Beneath his growls and howls, Cybela could be heard screaming and pleading. Talia released a blast that sent him tumbling over a pile of bodies and into a mud puddle.

Phalon raised his muddy face and screamed. Cybela shrieked like a banshee. Phalon crawled up from the muck. Gaining his legs, he sprang up and charged forward. Racing forward like a fired arrow, he leapt into the air aiming straight for Talia. His claws curled as tight as fishhooks.

Cyron broke into a frantic gallop driving on Talia and tackling her out of the way of the flying Wolfman.

Hanar stepped forward. "My father always said it was a good idea to share. This is for you, Phalon." Like a slingshot hurling a rock, he threw his last remaining exploding bottle. The small vial sailed through the air, heading for Phalon. The vial sailed toward his open mouth. When the bottle touched his lips, it exploded. The explosion tore Phalon's head from his body, turning it into mush. The rest of his body dropped like a rock of ice in a hailstorm, burying his remains in the muck.

Talia and Cyron looked up from their huddle to see Hanar covered in mud. He was staring down at what was left of Phalon with his fist clenched, a dark expression on his face, a smirk of satisfaction on his lips.

"What was that?" asked Talia standing and brushing herself off.

"One of Ladena's little surprises," Cyron answered with a half-smile. "Hanar, are you all right?"

"Better than I have been in a long time," Hanar responded with a sharp edge to his voice.

"Come on. Let's get to where the Centaurs are. Who knows what else is waiting for us in this place." Cyron and Talia started moving away.

Talia looked back and saw that Hanar was still standing, frozen in place. She returned and stood next to him.

"You've avenged your parents now, Hanar." She paused and bit her lip. "We've both done that. It's time to move on."

Holding out her hand, she took Hanar's hand in hers. Together, they hurried and caught up to Cyron.

CHAPTER 34

*I*n a clearing several hundred yards past the village, the Humans and the Centaurs faced each other across a grassy plain. The tension hung in the air, thick and sticky, like dampness before rain. The Humans grumbled and shuffled about like a hive of wet bees. The Centaurs cantered and clopped around like a nest of jostled wasps. No one made any advance toward the other. Each side stood their ground, lobbing angry looks at the other.

Sandwiched between the two angry swarms, a council was being held. Marreanus, the leader of the Centaurs, his son Tyrel, and their Shaman, Ladena, were on one side. The captain of the guard, Lucius, Lord Jannus of Alserra, and Hendrell, a representative from Mandoria, were on the other.

Lucius, his arm in a sling, and Marreanus, his white hair flagging in the wind, stood face to face. Their swords were planted in the soil before them as a sign of peaceful intent. The old guard talked as only warriors who have known battle can, without ceremony or façade. Despite the attitudes of their respective groups, the two shared a healthy respect for one another. Each not conceding ground, but not demanding it either, both aware of the realities that hot tempers never acknowledge.

"Are we to allow the temperature of our blood to rule the day or will cooler heads prevail?" Lucius asked, looking over Marreanus' shoulder at the anxious Centaurs.

"Our blood always boils for battle. I have lived long enough to know that battle for battle's sake is a sorry waste of a warrior," Marreanus replied.

"Well said. Our common foe is defeated. I do not wish to make or go in search of another," Lucius answered.

Marreanus nodded his agreement. "Neither do I. The complexities of life offer enough adversaries." He shuffled and settled into a contemplative stare. "Soon we will depart these lands. We make no claim on the Wolfmen's territory. When we have vacated what is now our home, you can claim that as well." He sighed and continued.

"This place offers us no future. It is better suited to the logic and mechanics of Man. We must return to where the world still believes in something other than itself, where there is no such thing as the impossible. Where magic and wonder still thrive."

"I understand. Our uneasiness with magic's mystery does not allow us to be comfortable with its possibilities." A silent understanding passed between them.

"Let me say in parting," Lucius puffed out his chest and stood at attention. "May our steel dance in battle, together or against, either would be an honor." He pressed his fist to his heart.

Marreanus' eyes brightened up. "This is a Centaur saying. There is no greater compliment one warrior can give to another."

"Yes," acknowledged Lucius. The two stared at each other for a moment, locked arms, nodded a bow, and then moved toward their waiting armies.

Ladena and Hendrell exchanged coded barbs, speaking the language of back door diplomacy and cloaked compromise. Both aged and learned, their words were an intricate play of secret agreements. Anyone hearing their conversation would assume they were talking about two different subjects.

"Tell your king," said Ladena. "…that he will have other children. A son and a daughter, in that order."

"This is highly unlikely. The queen is too mature to bear more children."

Ladena looked over her shoulder as she moved away. Smiling she said. "I said the king would have more children. I never mentioned the queen."

"Oh," Hendrell placed his hand to his mouth to cover the smile at the realization of what she said.

Tyrel and Lord Jannus assessed and reassessed each other while drifting in and out of the conversations of the others. They were two young future leaders unsure of the rules of the game, but curious to be included. They eyed each other suspiciously, but respectfully.

Emerging onto the clearing by way of a small hill, Talia, Cyron, and Hanar stood at the head of the two opposing forces.

Talia recognized the faces of many of the people of Mandoria. Some she had known all her life. Faces she had known to be pleasant were now twisted into scowls of anger. They were wielding all manner of weaponry. Some encrusted with the blood of the earlier fighting; others shining new, and anxious for action.

Cyron's attention went to the group of Centaurs spread out in their smudged armor with bows at the ready and the hilts of swords in their hands. They stepped in place as if they were fighting against a draw that was pulling them forward. Male and female warriors alike were eager for battle.

"This does not look good," Hanar said wagging his head.

"No, it does not," Talia and Cyron agreed turning their heads to focus on the other's group.

"What are we going to do? Do we pick sides?" Hanar asked.

No one dared break the silence with an answer. Tyrel finally noticed them on the hilltop and broke into a run to meet them. "Cyron," he yelled as he approached, a giant smile on his face. He stopped in front of Cyron and they locked arms in an embrace of solidarity. "I'm so glad you made it. I couldn't let you down again." He bowed his head, remembering past embarrassments. "We got here as soon as we could." He continued.

"It took some convincing, but Ladena and I finally talked my father and the council into joining the battle." He turned to acknowledge Talia and Hanar. "I'm happy to see you're free, Talia, and you too, Hanar." He gave them a hesitant smile.

'What's going on here Tyrel?" Cyron asked his brow furrowed with worry.

"We got here in just enough time to help the Humans finish off the Wolfmen. There were a lot more of those furry devils than we thought. If we hadn't shown up when we did, the Humans might have been wiped out. They were outnumbered and losing. Our numbers turned the tide. We joined forces and were victorious. It was glorious, Centaurs and Humans fighting side by side. Who would believe it?" A glow of great pride shined from his face.

"After we had won the day, more Humans showed up. Something happened, they turned on us. We've been at a standoff ever since." He looked back onto the field.

"I don't know what's going to happen. Maybe war." His expression turned hard and sharp.

"We fought with them and now they want to turn on us. You can't trust them."

"This is what you wanted, isn't it? I thought you hated the Humans." Talia asked.

"I don't hate...I mean...no...I...I"

Talia turned to Cyron. "We can't let them fight. We have to stop this before it begins."

Tyrel muscled his way in the conversation. "You don't stop Centaurs from battle. We are warriors. If there is going to be fighting, we will gladly do it."

"Hasn't there already been enough killing and destruction?" Talia asked.

"He's right, Talia. This may be unavoidable. It's been coming for a long time. I don't know if we can just talk this away."

"We'll see about that," she said, turning and marching toward the line of humans.

"Where are you going?" Cyron asked.

"To talk this away before some more killing starts."

"You can't go there." Cyron said catching up to her. "They think you killed Thangor, remember. If you go over there they'll..." Cyron shook his head. "One rescue a day is my limit."

"I won't need rescuing. I'll explain about Cybela. They've known me all my life. They knew Father." She scanned the crowd of faces. "Barnabus is surely there. He'll believe me. He'll make them understand."

"Talia," Hanar said, joining the conversation. "He's right. You can't risk it. What if they don't listen?"

"They will listen. I know it. They know me," her voice not as sure and clear as it was moments ago. "I'm going."

Talia straightened her back and marched toward the crowd. "Go and talk with Ladena and Marreanus. We can't let this happen." She yelled back.

"She's your sister," Hanar said. "Do something."

"How do you stop a storm?" Cyron asked.

Emboldened, Talia marched up to the crowd of grumbling men. "You can't start a war. The Centaurs don't want to fight you. If you..."

"Grab her!" somebody yelled.

"Hold her arms so she can't do her Witches' magic on us."

"Let me go. You don't understand!" Talia screamed as she struggled in the powerful hands holding her. "Barnabus! Where's Barnabus?"

Lucius held up a hand to dissuade the Centaurs from charging to Talia's rescue. "Let her go." He ordered entering the crowd. "I said, let her go!"

"She killed the prince!" A chorus of voices yelled.

"We must avenge Thangor!" Someone shouted.

"Careful she doesn't hex us," suggested another.

"She did not kill the prince. Remove your hands from her, or I'll remove your hands from you." Lucius raised his sword and presented it forward.

"But, Captain," the men released her and stepped away from the threatening steel. Talia stepped away from her captors and asked the captain, "Barnabus, where is Barnabus?"

"The king will have her head," someone said.

"If you let her go, he'll have your head too, Lucius." another added.

"Then he can have it." He took her arm leading her away from the crowd. "Come with me, Talia. There are things I must say to you." Alone, away from the crowd, he turned to her.

"I'm sorry Talia, but Barnabus is gone."

"What do you mean?"

"He's dead, Talia. He died in the dungeons at the hands of Cannullus."

"Uncle Barnabus gone? How could this happen?" Tears welled up, turning the world in a foggy haze. "First, he kills my father, and now Barnabus."

"Is he dead?" The captain asked, knowing the answer, but wanting confirmation. She did not answer. "Talia," he insisted. "Is Cannullus dead."

"Yes, he's dead!" she yelled. "And his pet Wolf, Phalon, too!"

The captain showed no surprise. "I see you have escaped the influence of the Shaman. I know that you did not kill Thangor, but the king holds you and magic responsible. In his anger and grief, he has banned all magic and those that practice it from the land. Hendrell came with his decree. You cannot return to Mandoria nor can you stay in Alserra. To remain in this realm would mean persecution and certain death for you."

Lucius' calm exterior gave way. "I tell you this because I respected your father. He was a fair and just man. I would not wish to see his daughter treated badly." He paused.

"Talia, there is no place for you or for magic anymore. The people are on the king's side. They fear magic. They fear you. To stay would be folly. Be safe. Go with the Centaurs."

"Barnabus dead. Magic gone. No. Why..." Talia's words trailed off. Anger and sorrow boiled in her. The power gathered and fell around her like the in and out of the tides. Talia looked into his downcast eyes, turned, and ran, stumbling forward until she collapsed in Cyron arms weeping.

"What's wrong, Talia? What did they do?" Her only answer was more tears.

CHAPTER 35

Talia was confined to the bed under the watchful eyes of her grandmother, Ladena. A debilitating fever left her delirious and weak. Talia cried, uncontrollably, for hours each day and spent fitful nights of troubled sleep. Disturbing visions and fitful delusions haunted her slumber. Images of Talleon and Barnabus caused her to cry out their names in heart-wrenching screams.

Specters of Thangor, Phalon, Cybela, and Cannullus produced involuntary bursts of magic that gathered around her, whipping the covers from her body, knocking things from the wall, and turning over the furniture as she struggled against them. Ladena forced potions and elixirs down her throat, trying to bring her back to health.

Cyron stayed by her bedside for hours each day, holding her hand, talking to her, and making plans about the things they would do together in the future. He promised her picnics in the secret garden and how he would teach her to shoot a bow and arrow. Often the bouts of pain she felt would become so intense they would reach out and bring him to his knees in shared agony. He constantly reached out to her mind.

Talia, I'm here. I will not leave you. Come back to us. Only silence answered back.

Hanar sneaked into the village every evening after dark and spent his nights sitting by her bedside, talking to someone who neither answered or acknowledged that he was there. He would patiently wait with her and wipe the sweat from her brow. Hanar recited to her, over and over again, the stories his father used to tell him, acting out each part, complete with voices. Every dawn he'd escape back to his hollow, only to return the next night.

"Ladena," Cyron asked. "Will she be all right? What can we do to help her?"

"I really don't know, Cyron. I have done all I can. Sometimes in one's life there can come a time when you are carrying too much. In the last few moons Talia has lost so much, she has been through so much. Many new things have opened up for her. She has seen the possibilities for her, their limitations, and most important, their costs, so like an overloaded wagon, she has broken down. Now she feels she is losing magic, the one constant thing in her life. The thing that is as much a part of her as her arms are." Ladena stroked her forehead.

"Will she be all right? I don't know. The gods willing..." The lines of worry on her face deepened and grew more pronounced.

"Hanar and I will do anything that we can to help her."

"This trial is hers. Talia will have to fight this alone. Just keep doing what you're doing, Cyron. It's good that you're here. She may not show it, but she knows you're here," Ladena added walking away. "She has strength she does not realize she has. I believe she will prevail when she realizes who she is. Then and only then will she return to us."

"There are only a few days left before we must depart. What about the girl?" Marreanus asked.

"She is still weak, but awake and recovering."

"There has been much discussion about her making the crossing. I fear she will not be allowed?"

Ladena knitted her brow. "Of course, she will."

Marreanus tilted his head and looked at Ladena from the corner of his eyes. "Is that the hopeful answer of a grandmother wanting to keep her child close or the truth from the Shaman of the clan?"

Marreanus' expression grew dark and serious. "The land lives and breathes for us, for our kind. There never has been any other. Only those of pure blood have been allowed. Our clan has accepted her, but the others will not. They will consider her an outsider, an insult, an abomination. We return by their grace and the grace of the gods. We cannot go against their will." Marreanus faced Ladena.

"This time I must be the one to give advice. You have an unhappy truth to face. A choice that really is not a choice at all. The clan does not exist without you. You cannot stay behind. No one knows this better than you. The gateway must be opened and sealed, by you. You know this." Marreanus cleared his throat. " She is not fully of the blood. The source will not..."

"I know this, Marreanus," she snapped. "Don't you think I have agonized over this? You need not lecture me on the nature of the gateway or the source." She began pacing in a circle.

"Cyron, he is not fully of the blood either. If she cannot enter, neither can he. Don't you know the nightmare of losing both Cyrenia's children has haunted me? Cyron, who I have cradled since he was a colt. This girl who has come into my life and stolen my heart. I know that when I enter the gateway I may never cross back again. And I know neither one of them can ever make the crossing." Ladena cupped her hands over her eyes.

"To choose between my grandchildren or my people." She sighed. "The gods can be truly unkind." She shook her head and looked to the skies. With a voice strained by despair, she asked, "How do I rip my family apart and break all our hearts?"

"Hanar, you can't leave. I'll miss you terribly. There must be a way for you to go with us."

"I will miss you too, Talia. You, Cyron, Ladena, and even Tyrel, have become like family. But Ladena says I will not be permitted to enter. I don't have Centaur blood. So..." he hunched his shoulders.

"With you leaving, there is no reason for me to stay here. I will go back to my hollow. I'm sure Capell has been there every day looking for me" Hanar twitched a half-smile.

"We've been through so much together. I can't imagine my life without you."

"It has been an exciting adventure. If you hadn't come along, I would have lived out my whole life in that hollow and never had this grand adventure."

"If you go back, you'll be all alone."

"I won't be alone. I still have my friends in the forest. I'll be all right. It's not safe for you here. You have to go. Besides, as much as I have grown use to Ladena and the others, living in a world with nothing but Centaurs makes me a little nervous."

Talia giggled and looked around to make sure no one else heard. "I'll admit even though they're my family, the thought does frighten me a bit, too." Hanar joined in. They laughed like naughty children sharing a secret.

"Talia cannot cross over with us. The source will not accept her. If she enters the land she will die before she places her feet on the other side."

"But, why, Ladena. She is of our clan. She is of our blood." Cyron asked.

"The gods granted the land to the Centaurs and to Centaurs only. The others and the source will not allow her in. She is too Human. She is not pure. It is the law. Our land is only for our kind. This is the Human world. She must remain here. It is our way. I am sorry, Cyron. If I could make it other than it is, I would. She cannot go."

"We cannot leave her behind Ladena. She's my sister. It would break her heart," Cyron mumbled to himself, "and mine."

Ladena yelled at him. "It is not your decision Cyron, or mine! Don't you think it breaks my heart also to know I must abandon Cyrenia's child, my child, for the sake of the clan. For the sake of ancient pride." Ladena fell back on her haunches as if the words had knocked her down.

"I don't know how I can tell her this. I don't know if I can find the strength."

"I will tell her. You need not bother. It will be better coming from me."

"Cyron, I..."

"I will do it, Ladena!" He yelled before barraging out the door. Cyron raced across the yard almost running over Hanar.

"Hey, watch where you're going." Cyron kept going without stopping or looking back.

"Cyron, Cyron." Hanar called after him. "Are you all right, Cyron?"

Cyron galloped out of the village, past the cemetery, and headed for the foothills. He did not stop until he reached the secret garden. He was kicking holes in the ground as he raged at the others for not accepting his sister. "I won't leave her behind all alone. I won't. I don't care what the others say."

Moments later Hanar fell into the garden, panting and out of breath. "Didn't you hear me calling you?" He huffed bending at the waist and placing his hands on his knees.

"Why did you follow me?" Cyron shouted.

"You looked like there was trouble and I wanted to help," he wheezed.

"There is nothing you can do. Go back and leave me alone."

Hanar plopped on the ground. "I'm too tired to walk back right now, so you might as well tell me what's wrong while I rest."

Cyron stamped around and kicked the apple tree. An apple fell and rolled toward Hanar. He picked it up and took a bite. "Thanks, I could use something to eat."

Cyron stomped around digging holes in the ground. "Talia can't go with us!" He finally shouted.

"Can't go with you? Why?" Hanar asked in mid-chew with a mouth full of apple.

"The others won't except her. They say she is too human. I don't care what they say. I'm not leaving her here alone."

"She won't be alone. I'll stay with her. I know it's not the same, but..."

Cyron hung his head. "I can't go, Hanar. If she can't go then I can't go. I have to stay here with her. She's my sister. I can't abandon her. She's already lost so much."

"Are you sure Cyron? This may be your only chance to go to the Land of the Centaurs."

"I'm sure," he took in a deep breath. "I always wanted to see it but..." he swallowed.

"Cyrenia used to tell me stories about her growing up there, but it's not my home. This is my world. What's left of my family is here."

"What about Ladena? Won't you miss her?"

"Yes, I will, but she has to go. The clan needs her. She belongs there. That is her home. This is our home. Talia and I will be all right here."

"Sure, you will and I'll be here too. I'm not going anywhere," Hanar said, burying his face in the apple.

"We've got to figure out a way to convince Talia to stay. I don't want her to know that they won't have her. It would hurt her too much. When you've lived your whole life being rejected, the last thing you want to hear is that it's happening again."

"How are you going to manage that without telling her the truth?" Hanar asked.

Cyron cantered around in circles. "Maybe if I tell her that I can't go, she'll decide to stay behind with me..."

"But, what reason could you give her? She knows how much you want to go."

"I don't know. Maybe Ladena can come up with something? We still have a few days before they leave."

Cyron kicked a stone into the pond. "Keep this to yourself Hanar. Talia can't find out."

"Don't tell me. She reads your mind, remember?"

Ladena began preparing the night before the crossing. She prayed, made the sacrifices, and invoked the necessary magic to open the gateway. A single dot of light appeared and began to grow. Through the night the dot grew to be brilliant doorway ten feet high and ten feet wide. When the sun rose between the mountain peaks the exodus began.

The procession started solemnly with the boxes holding the bones of the dead. Each in turn getting a pronouncement of their name, their family, and their victories in battle.

Next came the council, carrying scared scrolls of laws and prophecy and each declaring to the glory of the gods. The council was followed by the march of the elderly returning to the place of their origin. Everyone was clad in their best finery, carrying an emblem of their territory of birth. Heads were held high with the pride and dignity only the aged have earned. They paraded, chanting their lineage from a millennium in the past to the present.

Next came the young. Colts and foals of all ages and sizes, skipping into this new adventure and excited by the unknown. A contingent of females proceeded next, adorned in ceremonial dress and carrying the clan's prized possessions. They sang the song of homecoming taught to them from birth.

The warriors brought up the rear. Centaurs, male and female clad in their finest armor, carrying shields and spears, marched proudly into the vortex with metal gleaming like polished glass. Their voices were alive with songs recalling glorious battle, victorious triumphs, and the pride and honor to serve their clan.

By early evening, only Marreanus, Tyrel, Ladena, Cyron and Talia remained. It had been a long day of ritual and ceremony. Hanar had been standing off to the side, watching all day. Amazed by the spectacle, his mouth hadn't closed all day.

Tyrel stamped in place, anxious to get to the other side. "Come on, Father. It's our turn to go."

"Slow down young buck. It's not going anywhere." He turned to Ladena and an understanding passed between them. "I will see you on the other side." It was a question wrapped in a statement.

"Don't worry, Marreanus. It will be as it should be. Go along, I will only be a moment." Marreanus raised his brows, and then he and Tyrel entered the portal.

"Cyron," Ladena called. "It is time. I must be going. She pulled him to her, kissed him, and whispered in his ears. "I love you, my boy. I am so proud of you. I have always been proud of you. Take good care of your sister. She doesn't know her own power. You will have to be her anchor. Although I won't be here, I will be watching over you."

"Ladena, grandmother," were the only words he could manage to form. His throat was locked up with unshed tears. He hugged her as if he were a sponge absorbing water.

"No tears now, my brave young warrior. This is not goodbye. You will not get rid of Ladena that easily." She cupped his face in her trembling hands and smiled.

"Talia does not know yet that we are not going." Cyron said. "You have to play along with what I say." Ladena gripped his hand, closed her eyes, and nodded yes.

Talia was saying goodbye to Hanar. He stood wide-eyed looking like he was standing before a firing squad.

"Thank you, Hanar. I am so sorry you are not going. I will never forget you." She threw her arms around his neck and kissed him on the cheek.

Cyron walked up behind them. "Talia, I kept this from you until now because I didn't want to make you sad or have you try to talk me out of it. But, I cannot go with you. I have to stay behind."

"Stay behind? But, why?" The pitch of her voice rose with every word.

"Someone has to stay behind as payment for the members of our clan that did not die honorably. We drew lots and...ugh... I was chosen." His mouth twitched in a nervous smile. "It is an honor. I accept it proudly."

"Ladena!" she cried out running to her grandmother. "Cyron says that he is staying. Stop him Ladena. Don't let him do this." Her green eyes flashed with terror.

"It is our way, child. Cyron is a Centaur. He understands the ways of duty, honor and sacrifice."

"Pick somebody else. Please, not him." She cried.

"This is the way it is, Talia. We cannot change who we are. Now come. We must go." Ladena took her hand.

"No," she screamed pulling away. "If he stays then so will I." Her eyes were full of tears.

"It is time to seal the gate. We cannot wait any longer. Now come child." Ladena insisted.

"I will not leave him here alone." Talia shouted between her tears. She fell into Ladena's arms. "I cannot go with you if it means leaving my brother behind."

Ladena joined in her tears. "Very well, child." She whispered to her. "If that is your decision, then I must leave without you. Know that Ladena loves you." She squeezed her tighter.

"Take care of each other and remember what I have taught you." Ladena held her at arm's length and looked in her eyes. "Your magic is powerful and pure. Keep it that way. Guard it and it will do you well. Freeing yourself from Cybela was the mark of a true Sorceress. In order to be yourself you have to know who you are. You have proven that you do. I am very proud of you."

Her expression turned serious. "Cyron will need help with his gift. Since I will not be here to guide him, he will be counting on you. As will I."

Talia bit her lips and shook her head. Ladena walked toward the opening. She turned and looked at them, all three holding hands. "My children. I love you." She mouthed the words.

"You too, Hanar Knoll." He beamed and started crying. As Ladena entered the portal she yelled back to them. "I left you something special." The gateway swirled and with a whoosh, evaporated.

The three stood and looked at the empty space until the darkness overtook them.

CHAPTER 36

The next morning, Hanar prepared a meal. The three sat and stared at the food as if they didn't know what it was. The mood around the table was more funeral than breakfast. No one spoke. Their expressions were as vacant as the village was.

Talia sat for long hours counting her losses. She was wondering if this was to be her fate, to always lose the ones and the things she cared about. She had Cyron and Hanar, but had lost her father and lost a mother, without ever getting to meet her. Ladena was a welcome surprise, but she was gone too, as was Barnabus. They were all gone and her heart felt the void. She could never return to Mandoria because magic was outlawed in the kingdom. And she was wanted as a criminal.

What do I do? Where do I go? The sadness and confusion showed in the hollowness of her eyes.

Cyron wandered through the empty town reliving the years he'd spent there growing up. Never in his short life had he felt so alone. Everyone and everything he had cared about was gone, never to return. Fond memories played at him only to be replaced by the emptiness of his loss.

Hanar tried to lift their spirits by staying as cheerful as he could, but soon their drab moods began to drag him down as well.

Talia was fumbled around Ladena's house thinking of the grandmother she had lost. She ambled about touching and holding things, daydreaming about what could have been. Talia happened upon a large blue box and remembered Ladena's parting words: "I left something for you."

She opened the box. Inside she found Ladena's walking stick and a small black bag. Talia cradled the cane and hugged it to her breast. "I will never forget you, Grandmother. I love you. I'll miss you." In the black bag were three gold rings. When she touched the rings, she could feel the magic in them. The rings triggered a memory from her father.

"Heart rings," she shouted. *Of course, you would leave us some of your magic. Thank you, Ladena.*

Excitedly she called. "Cyron, Hanar, come here quick."

The two rushed in from their moping spots in the yard. "What's wrong? Why are you so excited?" Cyron asked.

"Ladena left these for us. If I'm right..." She handed each a ring. Her face beamed like a lantern. "Put them on," She insisted. "How she knew to make three, I don't know."

Cyron and Hanar shared a sidelong look.

"Ooh," Hanar purred. "That feels funny. What is it, magic?"

"I'm sure these are heart rings." Talia said.

"What so special about a ring?" Cyron mumbled.

Talia gave him a firm look. "I'll show you, grumpy." She guided them into a circle. "All right, extend your hand like this, palm up. Let our fingers touch."

"I don't feel nothing," Cyron said.

"Just a moment," said Talia. "Wait on it, wait on it, there." A jolt shot up all their arms. "There it is."

"What was that?" asked Hanar.

"We are joined. Now we can use the rings."

"Use them to what?" Cyron asked with a grouchy voice.

"We can use them to find each other in case one of us gets lost or something, but best of all we can do this..." she smiled, placing a finger to her chin.

'I'll need a bowl and some water." Hanar gathered a bowl and filled it with water. Talia had them sit in a circle around the bowl.

'Close your eyes and concentrate on Ladena. Think only of her." Cyron started to speak.

"Just do it," Talia ordered like a teacher scolding her pupil. They closed their eyes and after a few moments she said.

"Open your eyes." In the water of the bowl was the image of a pastoral land with lush green grass and blue skies. As they stared in amazement several Centaurs galloped by.

"That's Clavex and Toran and...and Dolgard," Cyron yelled, moving so close he upset the bowl and caused the scene to waver.

"Is that the land of the Centaurs?" Hanar asked.

"Yes," nodded Talia, wearing a smile too big for her face.

"Somehow Ladena had time to make these rings and enchant them with the necessary magic. These are heart rings. I read about them in one of Talleon's books. The ring allows whoever is wearing it to connect with the one another. It's like a window into their world. I don't know if these are powerful enough, but I read some are powerful enough that you can talk to them."

"Ladena," Cyron yelled, moving closer and upsetting the bowl again. Ladena turned around and winked at them.

"She knows we can see her. Ladena," he shouted again, finally managing to overturn the bowl completely.

"Oh, no. Get her back. Get her back." he pleaded. Cyron grabbed the bowl and refilled it with water, spilling half of it when he plopped it down. They repeated the process and regained the picture.

The rest of the day was spent sitting around the bowl and watching the Centaurs romp and play war games. Ladena nodded and blew them kisses. She called Tyrel to her side and he saluted them. Talia and Hanar smiled till their faces ached. Cyron wept like a baby.

"Maybe in the future, as the connection gets stronger, we can talk to her, but for right now we'll have to be happy with just seeing them."

"How long before we can talk to them?" Cyron asked.

"I don't know. We'll have to give it time and see." Talia said.

Talia and Hanar eventually retired for the night. Cyron sat in front of the bowl staring at the scene even when there was nothing to see but the night sky. Eventually, he dropped off to sleep, still sitting before the bowl.

The next morning was spent around the bowl again. "We can't spend the rest of our lives sitting here looking into this bowl," Talia said. "We have the rings. We can see them any time we want. As time goes by we will learn better ways to use them. They will keep us connected. Until then we have to do something with ourselves."

"What do you want to do?" Asked Hanar.

"We can't stay here. We're not wanted and besides there are too many bad memories here." Talia said.

"There are other places where we will be welcome." Cyron added. "We can travel like Talleon did when he was young."

"Where should we go?" asked Hanar.

"Let's go north," suggested Cyron. "I've always wanted to go to the Kingdom of Dyston in the Aarbees Mountains and see the Ice People. I've been told they are as tall as trees and carry great axes. The men are said to be great warriors who fight snow beasts with their bare hands. The women are supposed to be very beautiful with ice blue eyes, blue hair, and pale blue lips."

"I don't know about that. The idea of freezing my tail off just to see some Blue men fighting Snowmen doesn't sound like much fun to me."

"Icemen, Hanar, and they're fighting Snow Beasts."

"Whatever," shrugged Hanar. "I'd rather go to the south and see the Great River. My father told me it has no end. He said you could sail for moons on end and never reach the other side."

"That sounds exciting," chuckled Cyron. Let's go look at the water. Go stare at a giant wash tub."

Hanar twitched his nose at him. "Where do you want to go, Talia?"

Talia moved to the window. "I'd like to go to the east. To the other side of the Arganon Plains and visit the Land of the Celliphant. Talleon told me stories of that place when I was child. He said it was one of the finest places he ever visited. They live in houses made of crystals and sing their magic. Doesn't that sound lovely? Or maybe we could go west. To the Land of the Wind and find the Ramena. There's not much known about them. It is said they grow out of the ground like trees in their forest. Wouldn't it be exciting to be the first to see if that's true?"

"Sounds good to me. Let's leave in the morning. After a good night's sleep, we can decide which one we'll do first."

"That, my little Satyr friend, is the smartest thing you've said all day." Cyron attempted to pat Hanar on the head, but Hanar batted the hand away.

Cyron and Talia stood in the middle of empty village. "I'm glad you didn't pack more than you can carry easily." Cyron said. "We may have a long way to go before we can settle down for a while."

"It's hard to say goodbye to another home." Talia said looking around at the vacant houses.

"I know what you mean, but at least you're not going alone this time." Cyron reached out and took her hand. Hanar joined them, loaded down with baggage.

"That's too much stuff, Hanar."

"No, it's not." He answered. "It's mostly food. I get hungry when I travel."

"Alright, but you're carrying it, not me."

"It's alright, Hanar. Let me have one of those bags." Talia heaved the bag on her shoulder and proceeded down the lane.

Hanar took a deep breath and smiled. "Like my father used to say, "Today is yesterday's tomorrow, so tomorrow is day after tomorrow's yesterday.""

"What? That doesn't make any sense." Cyron said.

Hanar wrinkled his nose. "Just because you don't understand it doesn't mean it doesn't make any sense."

"I don't believe your father ever said any of those things. You made them all up, didn't you?"

"No, I did not. He did say them. My father was very wise."

"I'm sure he was too wise to say nonsense like that. You've been making up all those crazy sayings. Making us look silly believing you. Haven't you?"

"Tell him, Talia," Hanar pleaded. "You believe me, don't you?" They looked around for her. "Talia, Talia, where are you?"

Talia and Ladena's walking stick were down the road. The boys had to hurry to catch up with her.

"You did make them up. Admit it." Cyron insisted, cutting squinted eyes at the Satyr.

"No, I did not." Hanar answered. His cheeks puffed out.

"Yes, you did!"

"No, I did not!"

Boys, she thought shaking her head.

"He started it," Cyron answered.

THE END

ABOUT THE AUTHOR

Franklin R. Wilson is a retired engineer who found his writing voice later in life. Once he started writing, he hasn't stopped. *Hearts of Fire* is his second fiction book, and this book is the first of a series Franklin is planning.

You can find out more about Franklin and his books on his website.

www.ingramcontent.com/pod-product-compliance
Lightning Source LLC
Chambersburg PA
CBHW070004260626
47159CB00005B/1656